12 AMAZING SPORTS SHORT STORIES

Collected By: Dean Marra

2020

Copyright 2020 @ Dean Marra

TABLE OF CONTENTS

OLD WELL-WELL   7

WHEN I PLAYED BASEBALL   22

THE MIGHTY QUINN   25

FUNNY GIRL   32

HOBIE CAT DANGER   36

THE UNICYCLE AFFAIR   46

THE FREEKIN FREAK   54

THE LAST BOAT RIDE   65

SURPRISE LANDING   80

HOLE IN THE WALL   97

THE OTHER SIDE   107

FATHER'S EYES   130

INTRODUCTION

While great sports movies do not come along regularly, every so often one appears that absolutely takes your breath away. Cinema has the ability to take what we all love about sports: the spectacular moments, the drama, the grit, the teamwork and the determination, bringing it all together on the big screen.

Characters from Rudy to Rocky have us cheering on the edge of our seat come game time, yet it is not the games we remember most about sports flicks but the interactions between the characters themselves.

Who doesn't love that moment when the coach gets onto the chair with his team's back against the wall and inspires them to victory? Who doesn't love the look in the protagonist's eyes when he suddenly "turns it" on to mount a comeback?

It is these personable moments, which bridge the gap between the characters and the audience, that lead us to cheer so heartily for our favorite characters to succeed.

Here is a look at amazing sports short stories with the potential to become the next wave of unbelievable sports movies.

OLD WELL-WELL

By Zane Grey

He bought a ticket at the 25-cent window, and edging his huge bulk through the turnstile, laboriously followed the noisy crowd toward the bleachers. I could not have been mistaken. He was Old Well-Well, famous from Boston to Baltimore as the greatest baseball fan in the East. His singular yell had pealed into the ears of five hundred thousand worshippers of the national game and would never be forgotten.

At sight of him I recalled a friend's baseball talk. ``You remember Old Well-Well? He's all in--dying, poor old fellow! It seems young Burt, whom the Phillies are trying out this spring, is Old Well-Well's nephew and protege. Used to play on the Murray Hill team; a speedy youngster. When the Philadelphia team was here last, Manager Crestline announced his intention to play Burt in center field. Old Well-Well was too ill to see the lad get his tryout. He was heart-broken and said: `If I could only see one more game!' ''

The recollection of this random baseball gossip and the fact that Philadelphia was scheduled to play New York that very day, gave me a sudden desire to see the game with Old Well-Well. I did not know him, but where on earth were introductions as superfluous as on the bleachers? It was a very easy matter to catch up with him. He walked slowly, leaning hard on a cane and his wide shoulders sagged as he puffed along. I was about to make some pleasant remark concerning the prospects of a fine game, when the sight of his face shocked me and I drew back. If ever I had seen shadow of pain and shade of death they hovered darkly around Old Well-Well.

No one accompanied him; no one seemed to recognize him. The majority of that merry crowd of boys and men would have jumped up wild with pleasure to hear his well-remembered yell. Not much longer than a year before, I had seen ten thousand fans rise as one man and roar a greeting to him that shook the stands. So I was confronted by a situation strikingly calculated to rouse my curiosity and sympathy.

He found an end seat on a row at about the middle of the right-field bleachers and I chose one across the aisle and somewhat behind him. No players were yet in sight. The stands were filling up and streams of men were filing into the aisles of the bleachers and piling over the benches. Old Well-Well settled himself comfortably in his seat and gazed about him with animation. There had come a change to his massive features. The hard lines had softened; the patches of gray were no longer visible; his cheeks were ruddy; something akin to a smile shone on his face as he looked around, missing no detail of the familiar scene.

During the practice of the home team Old WellWell sat still with his big hands on his knees; but when the gong rang for the

Phillies, he grew restless, squirming in his seat and half rose several times. I divined the importuning of his old habit to greet his team with the yell that had made him famous. I expected him to get up; I waited for it. Gradually, however, he became quiet as a man governed by severe self-restraint and directed his attention to the Philadelphia center fielder.

At a glance I saw that the player was new to me and answered the newspaper description of young Burt. What a lively looking athlete! He was tall, lithe, yet sturdy. He did not need to chase more than two fly balls to win me. His graceful, fast style reminded me of the great Curt Welch. Old Well-Well's face wore a rapt expression. I discovered myself hoping Burt would make good; wishing he would rip the boards off the fence; praying he would break up the game.

It was Saturday, and by the time the gong sounded for the game to begin the grand stand and bleachers were packed. The scene was glittering, colorful, a delight to the eye. Around the circle of bright faces rippled a low, merry murmur. The umpire, grotesquely padded in front by his chest protector, announced the batteries, dusted the plate, and throwing out a white ball, sang the open sesame of the game: ``Play!''

Then Old Well-Well arose as if pushed from his seat by some strong propelling force. It had been his wont always when play was ordered or in a moment of silent suspense, or a lull in the applause, or a dramatic pause when hearts heat high and lips were mute, to bawl out over the listening, waiting multitude his terrific blast: ``Well-WellWell!''

Twice he opened his mouth, gurgled and choked, and then resumed his seat with a very red, agitated face; something had deterred him from his purpose, or he had been physically incapable of yelling.

The game opened with White's sharp bounder to the infield. Wesley had three strikes called on him, and Kelly fouled out to third base. The Phillies did no better, being retired in one, two, three order. The second inning was short and no tallies were chalked up. Brain hit safely in the third and went to second on a sacrifice. The bleachers began to stamp and cheer. He reached third on an infield hit that the Philadelphia shortstop knocked down but could not cover in time to catch either runner. The cheer in the grand stand was drowned by the roar in the bleachers. Brain scored on a fly-ball to left. A double along the right foul line brought the second runner home. Following that the next batter went out on strikes.

In the Philadelphia half of the inning young Burt was the first man up. He stood left-handed at the plate and looked formidable. Duveen, the wary old pitcher for New York, to whom this new player was an unknown quantity, eyed his easy position as if reckoning on a possible weakness. Then he took his swing and threw the ball. Burt never moved a muscle and the umpire called strike. The next was a ball, the next a strike; still Burt had not moved.

``Somebody wake him up!'' yelled a wag in the bleachers. ``He's from Slumbertown, all right, all right!'' shouted another.

Duveen sent up another ball, high and swift. Burt hit straight over the first baseman, a line drive that struck the front of the right-field bleachers.

``Peacherino!'' howled a fan.

Here the promise of Burt's speed was fulfilled. Run! He was fleet as a deer. He cut through first like the wind, settled to a driving strides rounded second, and by a good, long slide beat the throw in to third. The crowd, who went to games to see long hits and daring runs, gave him a generous hand-clapping.

Old Well-Well appeared on the verge of apoplexy. His ruddy face turned purple, then black; he rose in his seat; he gave vent to smothered gasps; then he straightened up and clutched his hands into his knees.

Burt scored his run on a hit to deep short, an infielder's choice, with the chances against retiring a runner at the plate. Philadelphia could not tally again that inning. New York blanked in the first of the next. For their opponents, an error, a close decision at second favoring the runner, and a single to right tied the score. Bell of New York got a clean hit in the opening of the fifth. With no one out and chances for a run, the impatient fans let loose. Four subway trains in collision would not have equalled the yell and stamp in the bleachers. Maloney was next to bat and he essayed a bunt. This the fans derided with hoots and hisses. No team work, no inside ball for them.

``Hit it out!'' yelled a hundred in unison.

"Home run!" screamed a worshipper of long hits.

As if actuated by the sentiments of his admirers Maloney lined the ball over short. It looked good for a double; it certainly would advance Bell to third; maybe home. But no one calculated on Burt. His fleetness enabled him to head the bounding ball. He picked it up cleanly, and checking his headlong run, threw toward third base. Bell was half way there. The ball shot straight and low with terrific force and beat the runner to the bag.

"What a great arm!" I exclaimed, deep in my throat. "It's the lad's day! He can't be stopped."

The keen newsboy sitting below us broke the amazed silence in the bleachers.

"Wot d'ye tink o' that?"

Old Well-Well writhed in his seat. To him it was a one-man game, as it had come to be for me. I thrilled with him; I gloried in the making good of his protege; it got to be an effort on my part to look at the old man, so keenly did his emotion communicate itself to me.

The game went on, a close, exciting, brilliantly fought battle. Both pitchers were at their best. The batters batted out long flies, low liners, and sharp grounders; the fielders fielded these difficult chances without misplay. Opportunities came for runs, but no runs were scored for several innings. Hopes were raised to the highest pitch only to be dashed astonishingly away. The crowd in the grand stand swayed to every pitched ball; the bleachers tossed like surf in a storm.

To start the eighth, Stranathan of New York tripled along the left foul line. Thunder burst from the fans and rolled swellingly around the field. Before the hoarse yelling, the shrill hooting, the hollow stamping had ceased Stranathan made home on an infield hit. Then bedlam broke loose. It calmed down quickly, for the fans sensed trouble between Binghamton, who had been thrown out in the play, and the umpire who was waving him back to the bench.

"You dizzy-eyed old woman, you can't see straight!" called Binghamton.

The umpire's reply was lost, but it was evident that the offending player had been ordered out of the grounds.

Binghamton swaggered along the bleachers while the umpire slowly returned to his post. The fans took exception to the player's objection and were not slow in expressing it. Various witty enconiums, not to be misunderstood, attested to the bleachers' love of fair play and their disgust at a player's getting himself put out of the game at a critical stage.

The game proceeded. A second batter had been thrown out. Then two hits in succession looked good for another run. White, the next batter, sent a single over second base. Burt scooped the ball on the first bounce and let drive for the plate. It was another extraordinary throw. Whether ball or runner reached home base first was most difficult to decide. The umpire made his sweeping wave of hand and the breathless crowd caught his decision.

``Out!''

In action and sound the circle of bleachers resembled a long curved beach with a mounting breaker thundering turbulently high.

``Rob--b--ber--r!'' bawled the outraged fans, betraying their marvelous inconsistency.

Old Well-Well breathed hard. Again the wrestling of his body signified an inward strife. I began to feel sure that the man was in a mingled torment of joy and pain, that he fought the maddening desire to yell because he knew he had not the strength to stand it. Surely, in all the years of his long following of baseball he had never had the incentive to express himself in his peculiar way that rioted him now. Surely, before the game ended he would split the winds with his wonderful yell.

Duveen's only base on balls, with the help of a bunt, a steal, and a scratch hit, resulted in a run for Philadelphia, again tying the score. How the fans raged at Fuller for failing to field the lucky scratch.

``We had the game on ice!'' one cried.

``Get him a basket!''

New York men got on bases in the ninth and made strenuous efforts to cross the plate, but it was not to be. Philadelphia opened up with two scorching hits and then a double steal. Burt came up with runners on second and third. Half the crowd cheered in fair appreciation of the way fate was starring the ambitious young outfielder; the other half, dyed-in-the-wool home-team fans, bent forward in a waiting silent gloom of fear. Burt knocked the dirt out of his spikes and faced Duveen. The second ball pitched he met fairly and it rang like a bell.

No one in the stands saw where it went. But they heard the crack, saw the New York shortstop stagger and then pounce forward to pick up the ball and speed it toward the plate. The catcher was quick to tag the incoming runner, and then snap the ball to first base, completing a double play.

When the crowd fully grasped this, which was after an instant of bewilderment, a hoarse crashing roar rolled out across the field to bellow back in loud echo from Coogan's Bluff. The grand stand resembled a colored corn field waving in a violent wind; the bleachers lost all semblance of anything. Frenzied, flinging action- -wild chaos --shrieking cries--manifested sheer insanity of joy.

When the noise subsided, one fan, evidently a little longer-winded than his comrades, cried out hysterically:

``O-h! I don't care what becomes of me-now-w!''

Score tied, three to three, game must go ten innings--that was the shibboleth; that was the overmastering truth. The game did go ten innings-eleven--twelve, every one marked by masterly pitching, full of magnificent catches, stops and throws, replete with reckless base-running and slides like flashes in the dust. But they were unproductive of runs. Three to three! Thirteen innings!

``Unlucky thirteenth,'' wailed a superstitious fan.

I had got down to plugging, and for the first time, not for my home team. I wanted Philadelphia to win, because Burt was on the team. With Old Well-Well sitting there so rigid in his seat, so obsessed by the playing of the lad, I turned traitor to New York.

White cut a high twisting bounder inside the third base, and before the ball could be returned he stood safely on second. The fans howled with what husky voice they had left. The second hitter batted a tremendously high fly toward center field. Burt wheeled with the crack of the ball and raced for the ropes. Onward the ball soared like a sailing swallow; the fleet fielder ran with his back to the stands. What an age that ball stayed in the air! Then it lost its speed, gracefully curved and began to fall. Burt lunged forward and upwards; the ball lit in his hands and stuck there as he plunged over the ropes into the crowd. White had leisurely trotted half way to third; he saw the catch, ran back to touch second and then easily made third on the throw-in. The applause that greeted Burt proved the splendid spirit of the game. Bell placed a safe little hit over short, scoring White. Heaving, bobbing bleachers-wild, broken, roar on roar!

Score four to three--only one half inning left for Philadelphia to play--how the fans rooted for another run! A swift double-play, however, ended the inning.

Philadelphia's first hitter had three strikes called on him.

``Asleep at the switch!'' yelled a delighted fan.

The next batter went out on a weak pop-up fly to second.

``Nothin' to it!''

``Oh, I hate to take this money!''

``All-l o-over!''

Two men at least of all that vast assemblage had not given up victory for Philadelphia. I had not dared to look at Old Well-Well for a long while. I dreaded the next portentious moment. I felt deep within me something like clairvoyant force, an intangible belief fostered by hope.

Magoon, the slugger of the Phillies, slugged one against the left field bleachers, but, being heavy and slow, he could not get beyond second base. Cless swung with all his might at the first pitched ball, and instead of hitting it a mile as he had tried, he scratched a mean, slow, teasing grounder down the third base line. It was as safe as if it had been shot out of a cannon. Magoon went to third.

The crowd suddenly awoke to ominous possibilities; sharp commands came from the players' bench. The Philadelphia team were bowling and hopping on the side lines, and had to be put down by the umpire.

An inbreathing silence fell upon stands and field, quiet, like a lull before a storm.

When I saw young Burt start for the plate and realized it was his turn at bat, I jumped as if I had been shot. Putting my hand on Old WellWell's shoulder I whispered: ``Burt's at bat: He'll break up this game! I know he's going to lose one!''

The old fellow did not feel my touch; he did not hear my voice; he was gazing toward the field with an expression on his face to which no human speech could render justice. He knew what was coming. It could not be denied him in that moment.

How confidently young Burt stood up to the plate! None except a natural hitter could have had his position. He might have been Wagner for all he showed of the tight suspense of that crisis. Yet there was a tense alert poise to his head and shoulders which proved he was alive to his opportunity.

Duveen plainly showed he was tired. Twice he shook his head to his catcher, as if he did not want to pitch a certain kind of ball. He had to use extra motion to get his old speed, and he delivered a high straight ball that Burt fouled over the grand stand. The second ball met a similar fate. All the time the crowd maintained that strange waiting silence. The umpire threw out a glistening white ball, which Duveen rubbed in the dust and spat upon. Then he wound himself up into a knot, slowly unwound, and swinging with effort, threw for the plate.

Burt's lithe shoulders swung powerfully. The meeting of ball and bat fairly cracked. The low driving hit lined over second a rising glittering streak, and went far beyond the center fielder.

Bleachers and stands uttered one short cry, almost a groan, and then stared at the speeding runners. For an instant, approaching doom could not have been more dreaded. Magoon scored. Cless was rounding second when the ball lit. If Burt was running swiftly when he turned first he had only got started, for then his long sprinter's stride lengthened and quickened. At second he was flying; beyond second he seemed to merge into a gray flitting shadow.

I gripped my seat strangling the uproar within me. Where was the applause? The fans were silent, choked as I was, but from a different cause. Cless crossed the plate with the score that defeated New York; still the tension never laxed until Burt beat the ball home in as beautiful a run as ever thrilled an audience.

In the bleak dead pause of amazed disappointment Old Well-Well lifted his hulking figure and loomed, towered over the bleachers. His wide shoulders spread, his broad chest expanded, his breath whistled as he drew it in. One fleeting instant his transfigured face shone with a glorious light. Then, as he threw back his head and opened his lips, his face turned purple, the muscles of his cheeks and jaw rippled and strung, the veins on his forehead swelled into bulging ridges. Even the back of his neck grew red.

``Well!--Well!--Well!!!''

Ear-splitting stentorian blast! For a moment I was deafened. But I heard the echo ringing from the cliff, a pealing clarion call, beautiful and wonderful, winding away in hollow reverberation, then breaking out anew from building to building in clear concatenation.

A sea of faces whirled in the direction of that long unheard yell. Burt had stopped statue-like as if stricken in his tracks; then he came running, darting among the spectators who had leaped the fence.

Old Well-Well stood a moment with slow glance lingering on the tumult of emptying bleachers, on the moving mingling colors in the grand stand, across the green field to the gray-clad players. He staggered forward and fell.

Before I could move, a noisy crowd swarmed about him, some solicitous, many facetious. Young Burt leaped the fence and forced his way into the circle. Then they were carrying the old man down to the field and toward the clubhouse. I waited until the bleachers and field were empty. When I finally went out there was a crowd at the gate surrounding an ambulance. I caught a glimpse of Old Well-Well. He lay white and still, but his eyes were open, smiling intently. Young Burt hung over him with a pale and agitated face. Then a bell clanged and the ambulance clattered away.

THE END

WHEN I PLAYED BASEBALL

By William Cline

When I was the age my oldest son is now, my mother made the claim that I ate, drank, and slept baseball. The subtleties of my mother's exaggerations aside, I know for certain that I did none of those things. I did play baseball every chance I got. I loved to play, like my son does now.

He is better at it than I ever was.

My mother goes to his games and watches him play just as she watched me play. Only now she sits in a fold-up lawn chair at the top of a slope beside the playing fields. When I played baseball she sat in the bleachers behind the backstop. From that position she was able to dispute the umpires calls - with uncanny accuracy, she claimed. Also from that position she found it impossible not to let every other parent at the park know exactly who her son was.

When I played left field, or center, I could still hear her hollering and yelling, and calling the umpires disparaging names, comparing them to unfortunates who had lost their ability to see.

At the top of the slope we sit and watch my son, her grandson, play. The fields are well manicured and fertilized to an emerald green. The pitcher's mound is a perfect elevated teardrop, and the infield grass has a checkerboard design mown into it by the parents who volunteer for such duty.

We can see the horizon from the top of that slope. We watch the clouds gathering from time to time, threatening to rainout the game. My mother complains about the rain, but I have become accustomed to it.

Games were never called because of rain when I played baseball. The grass in the outfield was always dry, its cut tips ragged and brown from the summer heat. The infield was hard baked clay with lumps of dirt and grass that made fielding grounders risky. The pitcher's mound sat in the middle, the white strip of the pitcher's rubber undercut by erosion, lopsided and scuffed by pitchers' cleats.

Occasionally the games would have to be stopped while a summer dust devil whirled along the base-paths, kicking up dirt and candy wrappers, moving in a random path from first base to third, until it finally danced into foul territory and died.

The game would go on; we would all trot back to our positions, our baggy uniforms flapping around our ankles and armpits. Our hands would sweat inside the leather of our mitts. Our baseball caps flattened our hair in a circle around our heads. We mopped our faces with our forearms.

The sun was always behind the base umpire, watching the play closely when someone would try to stretch a double out of a single. The sun and the umpire watched the slide and the tag, leather and cleats in a short race for the white canvas of the base. Then there was apprehension and quiet as the two players looked up for the umpire's call. Above them the umpire made his decision, but always there was the sun, above and behind everything, watching the play, never letting anything go unnoticed.

Today they play in polyester, very thin and cool. My mother always comments on how my son looks so sharp in his uniform.

These days I sit close enough to mom to benefit from her umbrella. I watch the clouds between innings, and wonder, only for the moment, where they were when I played.

The clouds are indifferent to the game, and to me. They and could care less about singles and doubles, leather and cleats, and the arbitrary calls of umpires. And when the rain quits, and mom puts her umbrella away, the one constant of the game returns, the one truth which will never be taken away from baseball by the sun, or by the gathering of clouds: my mother yelling at the umpires, making references to the blind.

I can hear her voice, echoing across the fields, and it makes me smile.

THE END

THE MIGHTY QUINN

By Lea Sheryn

I

By every account, Quinn Madison was a typical All-American Girl. In her bedroom, a poster of Andy Gibb was taped on her closet door; a giant Holly Hobby doll sat comfortably on the seat of her white rocking chair. Along with her best girlfriends, Helena, Samantha and Phoebe, she had seen the movie GREASE more than twelve times. They all loved John Travolta and absolutely wanted to grow up to become Olivia Newton-John. It was the spring of 1979. Boys were expected to be boys; mother's crossed their fingers hoping their girls still expected to be girls.

Twelve-year-old Quinn loved everything about her life. Although she was by every means an average child, the one thing she loved most of all was BASEBALL. Beneath her canopy bed was hidden a shoebox full of baseball cards. In the evenings, when she was supposed to be asleep, the box would come out of hiding. Sitting cross-legged with the pillow propped behind her and the comforter snuggly covering her lap, she memorized the stats on each and every card. Baseball was her passion; baseball was her life.

Early on a Saturday morning, Quinn woke up long before anyone else. Dressed in day-glo purple shorts with white piping around the legs and a matching t-shirt with a large white number 2 on the back, she rode her bike to the local schoolyard. Her bike was metallic red with a matching banana seat and red, white and blue streamers blowing happily from the ends of the handlebars. The white basket on the front was full of baseballs; her glove and ball cap rested on top.

Sure, she had played on the Girls' Softball Team the year before but underhand pitching just wasn't fast enough for Quinn. She wanted to feel the weight of a baseball in her hand; she wanted the thrill of the Fast Ball and the crack of the bat. Parking her bike next to the pitcher's mound at the school's ball field, she lifted her glove from the basket full of balls and inhaled the scent of freshly worked leather. Placing her cap on to her head, she was ready to go.

The ball in one hand, the glove fitting snugly on the other, Quinn assumed the position, raised both hands above her head, smoothly lowed them and released the ball. Too wide. Frowning, another ball was released. Too high. Again and again, a ball was released until the pitch was perfect.

Morning was slowly creeping toward noon as the girl became one with the ball and glove. By twos and by threes, little boys with baseball on their minds began to show up at the field on their own bikes. Many of them lined up outside the fence to stare at the strange sight that met them. Their minds screamed the same thought: GIRLS WERE NOT SUPPOSED TO PLAY BASEBALL!

II

"What's going on?" Buford Brown wondered as he rode his bike toward the schoolyard. "Why weren't the boys on the field tossing practice balls?" Standing on tiptoes, he craned to see what was going on as he balanced his own banana seat between his legs. What he saw nearly knocked him for a loop. Who was that girl who was pretending to be a pitcher?

Throwing his ride to the ground, fourteen-year-old Buford, better known to his friends as Buster Brown, stalked across the grassy field to confront the girl. As he drew closer, he recognized the honey brown ponytail sticking through the hole in the bottom center back of the purple ball cap perched on her head: Quinn Madison! One of the "Silly Sisters", he thought to himself as he approached the mound. Well, he thought, he would just have to send her back to the quartet of Quinn, Helena, Samantha and Phoebe. There would be a clear understanding: BASEBALL WAS FOR BOYS!

Just as Quinn was about to let go of the ball, Buster Brown stepped in front of her. Grabbing her arm, he roughly forced her to drop it. "GO HOME!" he yelled directly into her face.

Without blinking, Quinn bent down, retrieved the ball and sent it flying in a direct line across Home Plate. Buster had no choice but to step aside. A second ball sailed past him; the third narrowly missed his nose. Now he was all attention: This Girl Could Pitch! Without another word, he pulled his worn out catcher's mitt from his back pocket and strode toward Home Plate to assume the position.

III

Skeptically Quinn watched Buster Brown amble toward Home Plate. He was a big boy; not what one would consider fat or obese but rather what was referred to as hefty. As he squatted into position, she took in the pouch that hung over his belt and his thick thighs. Clearly, he wasn't one of her favorite people but he was there and she wanted to play ball. As soon as he lowered his catcher mask and punched his fist into his mitt, she let loose. The ball hit the mitt with a thud.

The pitches came in high and low, left and right, and dead center. Quinn threw; Buster caught. It was a cat and mouse game to see who faltered first. Neighbor boys leaned against the outfield fence or stood spellbound with their bikes between their knees. They had never seen anything like it. Without warning, the cat and the mouse suddenly became a team.

When it finally came to picking teams, Quinn was Buster's first pick. Thad Johnson, the other team captain, was disappointed at first but settled on Tommy McNeil as his pitcher. Back and forth, the scratch team was picked until each had a full squad. All the kids were accounted for; they all knew their positions from past Saturday games. The only newcomer was the girl.

The Game was On! By the time it was over, the fence line was full of spectators. In a small town word gets around fast. Men, women and children all heard there was a girl playing in the scratch game and rushed to see whom it was. Quinn's mother, Jenny Madison was all for marching onto the field to march her daughter home but her father, Frank, held her back. Her elder brother, Marvin, was in awe at her skill; he always admired his little sister's spunk.

It was a hard fought game, both teams were nearly equal, but Team Buster won the day, 6 to 4. From the mound, Quinn whipped her hat from her head and dropped it to the ground. Her long honey colored hair had lost it's ponytail somewhere around the third inning so it hung free around her face. She was grinning from ear to ear. Laughing, shouting and waving their arms in glee, Helena, Samantha and Phoebe rushed the field. Their best friend was the hero of the day and, without hesitation, they wanted to be a part of it.

IV

When Little League tryouts began, Buford Brown was the first to show up. He wasn't surprised to see Quinn Madison show up as the second. Never, in the history of the town, had a girl arrived on tryout day. "So she's going to play," Buster thought to himself. He couldn't help but grin from ear to ear. This was one Silly Sister who wasn't so silly in his opinion. He had realized a great respect for this skinny little girl.

Without much thought, the high honchos of the Little League world dismissed Quinn without given her a chance to prove her self. In their minds: GIRLS DIDN'T PLAY BASEBALL! The disappointment was evident in the girls face as she turned to walk away. Her shoulders sagged, her glove hung limply from her hand. She wanted to play! Damn boys and damn men who thought that girls couldn't play baseball, she thought as she headed for her bike.

"Hey! Are you stupid?!" Buster Brown yelled out as he rushed the men who were the deciding factor on who could play and who couldn't. Adamantly he advocated on Quinn's part. She was the best damn pitcher he had ever played with, he exclaimed. Finally he shouted: "If Quinn doesn't play, neither do I." Throwing his catcher's mitt down in a fit of rage, he stormed away.

Buster Brown was the Little League Star of his division and the Powers that Be knew it. They charged Buster and brought him back to reason with him. After a heated exchange, Quinn was brought back too and allowed to tryout. There was no question: she was on the team.

What a season! The bleachers were full at every game. Quinn was a star! Game after game was won by the combined efforts of Quinn and Buster. When she walked out onto the field, the home side spectators shouted out: "You'll Not See Nothing Like the Mighty Quinn!" Somehow the girl knew it was her father, Frank, who had started the chant. Still, she loved and basked in every moment of it.

V

Sooner or later, every child outgrows Little League but they rarely outgrow baseball. Quinn was the same. Her Little League days behind her, she moved onto to the High School team. There was no problem with her joining the team. By this time, all the coaches knew: if Quinn didn't play, Buster wouldn't play either. They were, by this time, practically an unbeatable team. Baseball, Buster and Quinn were words that all went together in the minds of the townspeople; you couldn't have one without the other.

Quinn grew into a beautiful, vivacious teenaged girl. Her hair grew longer and the honey color became richer. Buster lost his baby fat and became a tall, lean, muscular young man. No longer did he want to be referred to as "Buster Brown"; his name was Buford, therefore he wanted to be known as Bo. It seemed natural that the pitcher and the catcher should become a couple.

At the end of Bo's Senior Year, he took Quinn to the prom. Much to the surprise of the couple, they were elected King and Queen of the Prom. Since Quinn was only a sophomore, rules had to be broken but no one wanted to split up the "Dream Team". No one complained. On the stage, they were presented with their crowns and a glove and a mitt and a bat... Cheers resounded around the gymnasium.

Alas, the magic was over when high school was over for Quinn. Although she had been able to play baseball through her school days, no college would entertain a girl pitcher. Bo was able to continue to play; he was signed into the minor league at first but was soon in the Majors. Quinn had to content herself by being his #1 fan. Still, she wasn't worried. The next year, she became Mrs. Bo Brown, All-American.

THE END

FUNNY GIRL

By Dave Lane

The game of softball has always been entertaining and fun for me. As my age started to catch up with me and unable to keep up with the younger players, I decided to continue to be involved with softball as an umpire. Over the years in my new part time profession, I started to develop a thick skin. As an umpire you find out just how many critics are out there during a game. Parents and coaches all had something to say about a particular call I made. But none of them would ever bother to become a certified umpire. Listening to these remarks I would just shrug them off and continue with the game. There are times I would pull the coach aside and give them a warning and 95% of the time that would be enough to stifle any further remarks. In 16 years as an umpire, I have only thrown out three people, two coaches and a parent. All three were well deserved. During one game, I was not expecting this from a player.

It was a chilly April day in Massachusetts and I was working behind the plate at a local varsity high school game. The home team had this tremendous pitcher, she was ranked 2nd best pitcher in the state the previous year and she lead the state and strike outs with her speed and movement. Watching her warming up was impressive, you could hear the sharp "pop" of the ball hit the catcher's mitt. During the game her velocity was even more impressive. Her mechanics and complete control of the ball was simply beautiful. The opposing team's batter could not keep up with her speed and were completely fooled by the movement she had on the ball.

During the game, one batter after another was sent back to the bench. On occasions a batter might foul it off or hit a ground ball, but the infield was solid and made some nice plays. Only one batter made it safely to first base on a little blooper to left center, just out of the reach of the shortstop. Even in the late innings of the game, this pitcher still threw with the same intensity as she did in the first inning. The velocity and the movement of the ball never diminished. The top of the fifth inning had started with the pitcher still having complete control of the hitters. The first batter struck out on five pitches and the second batter went down swinging on three pitches. The third batter came up to the plate. Digging her cleats into the dirt, the batter took her position in the batter's box. My right hand was up and my arm extended out, like a police officer holding up traffic, waiting for the batter to get ready. When the batter settled into her spot in the batter's box I pointed toward the pitcher indicating we were ready. The first pitch came in fast, but low and outside. In a low tone I said, "Ball!" The second pitch was the same, low and outside, again in a low tone, "Ball!" The third pitch looked to be coming inside but at the last moment broke right over the plate, knee high. I yelled, "STRIKE!" and then came up with my with my arm raised and made a fist.

Batter looked at me and asked, "Time Blue?"

I yelled out, "Time!"

She stepped one foot out of the batter's box and took a couple of practice swings. Placing her foot back in and taking her position, I adjusted my stance behind the catcher. Raising my hand up I pointed at the pitcher to let her know we were ready to continue. The pitcher stood there and waited for the signal from the catcher and with a slight nod, she stepped up to the pitching rubber and began her wind-up. I crouched down behind the catcher and immediately picked up the ball as soon as it left her hand. This bright optic yellow ball appeared to be coming right down the middle of the plate, but it suddenly broke inside about two feet from the batter. The batter had started her swing and quickly realized at the last second the ball was going to jam her inside. The ball came in tight and crowded her, but she managed to catch a piece of the ball.

As an umpire, we are trained not to move or flinch from the ball, even if the ball is heading right for you. I did not move an inch, I had a tremendous amount of faith in the catcher that day and was anticipating her to block the ball. However in this situation, no one had enough time to react. The bat caught just enough of the ball to redirect it past the catcher's mitt and for some reason the ball seemed to accelerate from 50mph to light speed. In that instance I heard a loud bone crushing CRACK, and then felt an enormous amount of pain. The ball had hit the bone in my elbow and the pain radiated throughout my entire arm. The first words out of my mouth were not "FOUL BALL" or "DEAD BALL", but more on the side of profanity: "AHHHH SHIT!" I screamed out holding my left elbow. Dead silence took over the field. No one said a word, none of the coaches, fans or players. I could feel all eyes were on me. The catcher turned around with a blank look on her face, the batter had a look of horror on her face and the pitcher came running in saying, "I'm so sorry!" Finally the silence broke when someone yelled out, "Are you OK Blue!"

"Yea", I replied, but I wasn't. I could still feel the pain emanate in my left arm.

My partner on the bases came running from the first base side and as he approached me he said, "Damn! I heard that one from first base."

Making a fist with my left hand, I took a couple of deep breaths. The pain was starting to lessen, but not fast enough. I knew my elbow was going to kill me later tonight. Getting myself together I reassured the pitcher, catcher and batter that it was no one's fault. It really is just part of the game. The ball was tossed back into the catcher and she flipped it back to the pitcher. The catcher turned her head around as if to say "Are you sure you are OK?" I nodded my head and she took her position behind the plate batter. I stepped in behind her and was ready to continue. The third base coach called out to me, "Hey Blue what's the count?"

I looked down at my indicator and saw two balls and two strikes. I rose up my left hand, holding up two fingers and the same with the right hand and yelled back, "TWO BALLS AND TWO STRIKES!" It was at that moment I heard the catcher say "AND ONE AH SHIT!"

Funny Girl!

THE END

HOBIE CAT DANGER

By Gordon England

The summer of 1979 was wicked hot in Fort Worth, my new hometown after graduating from college. The only escape from the heat was for a few hours at one of the area lakes, preferably on a boat. Which I did not have, but somebody had a small Hobie Cat parked in my apartment parking lot. I'd never been sailing, but any kind of water craft perked my interest in that heat. I watched a neighbor about my age polishing the sailboat's two thin rudders one Saturday morning.

Sailors love to maintain their boats, so I asked him, "You need some help?"

"Sure, I'm taking her out today. My name's Ben."

"I'm Gordon. I just moved in upstairs."

We shook hands. His blond hair hung below his ears and a dark tan indicated much time on the water.

"How often do you polish those rudders?"

"Every time I go out." He noted my look of surprise. "I want them to be as sharp and smooth as a knife. Better speed that way. I wax the hull every couple of months too."

Interesting. I can't remember ever waxing dad's powerboats.

"Would you help me hook up?"

I guided him as he backed his truck up. When the bumper was close, I lifted the trailer and dropped it on the hitch.

Ben came back and tightened up a few lines. I noted the sleek design of two thin pontoon hulls, crossbars with a cloth mesh between the pontoons, and a mast and sail at the front crossbar. Barely a boat in my opinion.

"This sure is a light boat. How long is it?" I asked.

"Sixteen feet and only 340 pounds. I race it, so the lighter it is, the faster I sail."

"I didn't know they raced Hobie Cats. How fast does she go?"

"A bit over 20 knots," he said with a twinkle in his eye. "You ever been on one?"

"No." Please ask me.

"Have you ever sailed?"

"No, but I'd like to learn."

"Do you want to go now? I'm headed over to Lake Grapevine to do some practicing. There's a good wind today."

Jackpot. "Oh yes."

"I gotta warn you. She flies, and I spend most of my time up on one hull."

I wasn't sure what he meant, but said, "Count me in."

A few hours later we raised the mast, pulled the sail up, and pushed the Hobie into cool lake water. The sail stretched tight in a strong breeze, propelling us away from shore. We initially sat on the trampoline (the mesh between the hulls) while Ben gave me a rundown on sailing basics. There are no ropes on boats. Call them lines. The sail catches wind for speed and is controlled with a line connected to the mast crossbar. Wires connect the top of the mast to the pontoons for stability at several locations. A sharp rudder drops below the rear of each hull. Steer by adjusting a tiller connected to the rudders. When changing directions (tacking), the sail would swing across the boat. Our body weight would balance the craft to keep the wind from flipping it over.

"Put this harness on for sitting in your trapeze seat," he said. "It's also a life jacket."

I slipped the harness on and asked, "Why do I need a trapeze seat?"

"For sitting beyond the edge of the hull."

I looked at the water beyond the hull. "Why would we sit out there?"

"You're a novice," he said with a chuckle.

He untied two lines connected to the top of the mast and clipped one to his harness.

"Connect this to your harness," he said. "If you slip or we flip over, you'll stay with the boat."

Falling off was not in my plan, though hanging off the hull sounded interesting. I liked daring sports.

"Make sure your trapeze line doesn't tangle with the mast lines," he added. Hmm.

"We'll sail easy for a while," Ben said as he tightened the sail and adjusted the tiller to gain modest speed.

I moved around, getting a feel for the wind, pontoon balance, and water passing two feet below me. Unlike a noisy powerboat, only the sounds of the fluttering sail and hulls slicing through water broke the peaceful quiet of the lake. Nice.

"Coming about," Ben announced. "Watch out for the boom and stay in front of the mast so that your trapeze line doesn't catch the sail."

Yes, that would be a problem. He pulled the tiller to turn the rudders. The sail fluttered as the Hobie swung into the wind, rotating the crossbar toward the other pontoon. I ducked and scrambled on hands and knees across the rear of the craft to the opposite hull, then turned around to watch Ben effortlessly slide across the trampoline, keep multiple lines clear, and settle in next to me while not losing his grip on the tiller. The sail snapped tight, pulling the Hobie to a new course. Ben adjusted the sail line and tiller, then smiled at me.

"That wasn't so hard, was it?" he said with a big smile.

"No. I bet it can get pretty hairy with big wind."

"Yes." He chuckled. "Now we're going to push the speed up by sitting back on the trapeze and pulling the sail tighter."

"Okay."

"Watch me first, then you sit back."

Ben tightened the sail line to increase the force resisting the wind. I felt the hull rise under me, increasing our speed as the mast tipped slightly toward the water. I intuitively knew that if we rose too high the boat would flip. Ben stood up on the pontoon and leaned back while keeping a firm grip on the sail line and tiller. When the hull started to drop, he pulled the sail line tighter and our speed increased until reaching a balance with the windward hull one foot out of the water and the mast slanted about 30 degrees. I looked around, wondering how I would jump off if it flipped. This really was living on the edge.

"Your turn."

I carefully stood on the trampoline and pulled in the slack of my mast line, then leaned back against the tight line for balance. I back stepped onto the pontoon and released line to lean backward. The pontoon under my feet dropped, but Ben adjusted the sail and rudders to keep us above the clean blue water. Wow. I was doing it.

"Good move, Gordon. Now relax, you're all tensed up. Bend your knees and let them bounce with the boat. Just hold on to the line lightly."

Yes. This was like riding a horse with bent knees to keep my head level. No pull with my arms, just the casual hand pressure to keep from rocking side to side. Now the Cat sped through the water as my hair fluttered and small waves sizzled where sliced by the pontoon. And rudder.

"Coming down," Ben said after a few minutes. He slowly released the sail, dropping the pontoon into the water as I pulled on my line to stay standing. "How did you like that?"

"Almost as fun as racing motocross, but more lines and rudders and sails to keep track of."

He nodded, "I've been racing a couple of years now."

"How far is a race?"

"There are buoys at each end of the lake that we sail around. There are different classes and lengths of races. Something for everyone."

"I thought sailing would be easy. Just sit back and let the wind blow you around. But you have to be on alert every minute."

"Right. To go fast is difficult. The wind and waves change, other boats cut you off and steal your wind. For the highest speed, you lay that sail over to the fine line just short of rolling her over. Ready to go again?"

"Let's do it."

"Just don't make any fast moves."

Ben took us to the end of the lake, turned around with our back to the wind, and away we sailed. He tightened the sail line with one hand, controlled the tiller with another, and used his balance for leaning back. The hull rose and we leaned away the hull. It was hard enough for me to stay on top of the pontoon using both hands on my mast line. I didn't know how he concentrated on so many things at once.

After a few hundred yards at a fast clip, Ben said, "I'm going to push it a little more. Move closer to the front to balance our weight."

I held onto my line and wondered how much further he could raise the pontoon. Sure enough, it rose a few more inches. Water flew by faster. Best not to look down. I watched the sail angle increase slowly as Ben milked the wind for every bit of speed. Almost 45 degrees. At least 20 knots. He pulled the sail harder. I wondered who would give out first, him or the sail.

The wind decided the contest with a surprising gust that drove the sail all the way into the water. The Hobie stopped immediately, but Ben and I kept going 20 miles an hour, flying forward past the mast until we reached the end of our harness lines. We jerked to a stop and splashed into water next to each other. I popped to the surface and encountered a maze of lines, sail, and mast. One pontoon floated on its side in the water, with the other propped eight foot into the air. Ben thrashed beside me.

"Damn wind tricked me. That's the first time I've rolled this year. Unhook your line and swim away from the mast. Don't worry, the sail will keep the mast from sinking."

That was heartening. This was my first time to flip a boat and I didn't want to go down with it. Though I did enjoy the cool lake water. We untangled ourselves from the lines and swam to the other side of the boat. Ben climbed onto the pontoon in the water, snatched a trapeze line, and threw it over the other pontoon. We grabbed the line and pulled hard to raise the sail upright.

"Good work, Gordon." Ben high fived me.

"Let's do it again," I said. "Without flipping it."

"Okay. You get in front of me this time, by the lead crossbar."

We attached our trapeze lines and angled the boat across the lake, raising and lowering the windward pontoon up and down. I found that balancing the sail at about 45 degrees maximized our speed. The challenge was staying at the far edge. As the boat approached the shoreline, Ben unexpectedly loosened the sail and jolted the boat. Caught off-guard, my feet slipped, and arms wind milled. I knew what would happen next, so I took a deep breath as I fell in front of the trampoline and splashed between the pontoons. I reached the end of my trapeze line when I was two feet under water. The line jerked tight against the crossbar that still moved at 20 miles an hour. Trapped at speed under water, I spun helplessly at the end of the line. Ben released the sail to drop the airborne pontoon and stop the boat. My submerged thrashing ended in seconds, but it felt like minutes to me.

Ben laughed as I awkwardly climbed back onto the trampoline, coughing up water. "We had really good speed there for a while. You're learning. Ready for another run?"

"No, but we have to get back to the other side of the lake, so I'm good for one more time. This time you ride up front and I'll be toward the rear. If I fall in, the boat won't catch my line and drown me." We sorted out the lines and prepared for another ride.

A brief time later, the Cat rose up on one pontoon again as we leaned back. I must admit that riding high up on a hull above the water was thrilling. We were just about back to the boat ramp when a series of gusts of devious wind shook the boat. I balanced through the first gust, but the next one caused my feet to slip again. Down I dropped between the pontoons. I opened my eyes under water just in time to see the end of a pontoon pass over me. The sharp rudder sliced the water at 20 miles per hour just inches from my face. I screamed under water in terror.

Ben stopped the boat and pulled me in.

"Are you okay?"

Choking and spitting, I climbed onto the trampoline and lay on my back. "That rudder damn nearly cut my head off."

He laughed.

"You sharpen those for quick death, don't you?"

More laughter.

"I've had enough. Let's take her in on both pontoons. I'm staying on the tramp. No more of your high-speed tricks."

"Oh, come on Gordon. You'll get the hang of it. You can be my racing partner."

"I got news for you. This is my last time on a catamaran. And probably a sail boat too. It's too much work and not enough fun. We worked hard the whole time screwing with lines and sails and wind and crashing. I used up one of my nine lives and want to keep the rest of them."

And that was the last time I was foolish enough to sail a Hobie Cat.

THE END

THE UNICYCLE AFFAIR

By Gordon England

"We're going to have a problem next year with the tumbling team," I told my blond curly haired best friend, Steve Craig.

"Why is that?"

Steve and I were lowly freshmen at Richardson High School in Dallas that spring of 1969. I had been on Coach Spangler's private tumbling team for three years. We worked out before school started in the morning at the high school gym with boys and girls of all ages. In those days we mostly performed on the trampoline and tumbling on mats. The team traveled around north Texas and Oklahoma performing acrobatic shows for county fairs, college and professional basketball game half time acts, and Dallas Cowboy pregame shows.

"This was your first year, so you probably didn't pay much attention to the older guys on the team," I said.

"No, not really. I was just trying to get good enough to make the team."

"Remember our clown, Tom?"

"Yeah. He kept diving over people on the ground and falling off the trampoline."

"He graduated and we won't have a clown next year," I said.

"Can't he still be on the team?"

"You didn't hear. He and the other seniors were drafted to go to Vietnam," I replied.

"Oh."

"Coach says we need to come up with a new act."

"Hmm. What could that be?"

"I was thinking."

"That usually gets you in trouble," Steve said with a grin.

"That's the fun of it. Anyhow, I went to the traveling circus last winter and everyone loved the clown on the unicycle."

"Uh oh."

"Yeah man. Wouldn't it be cool to learn to ride one for the team?"

"You know it. But we don't have a unicycle," Steve pointed out.

"Not yet. But I have a birthday coming up in May. I'll ask Mom for one."

Steve grinned. "Good idea."

"If I learn to ride it, you will have to also."

"No problem. I can do anything you can."

He was right about that. In his first year on the team, Steve had already learned most of my trampoline tricks. We spent hours after school practicing on the trampoline in my back yard with the other kids in the neighborhood. I would dare him to try a new flip and he got up there and had it down in no time. He was a natural trampolinist.

"How tall a unicycle are you thinking about?"

"Hmm. Taller is cooler," I said with a grin.

"Taller is also further to fall down."

"Right. I always say don't go higher than you want to fall. I'll get the short three-footer."

When my birthday rolled around, I became the proud owner of the only Schwinn unicycle in town. The next day, Steve and I wheeled it out to my driveway and looked at it with curiosity.

"How are you going to get on it, Gordon? That's not like a bicycle."

"Well." I lifted the seat up over the wheel and let go. Down it crashed.

"Do you meant it didn't come with training wheels?" Steve snickered.

"No handle bars either." It dawned on me that I would not be able to climb on it like a bike. No problem. I took it to a wall so I would have something to hold onto. Hmm. The wheel and seat were situated such that to sit on the seat, my feet would be six to fifteen inches off the ground. I couldn't just step onto the pedals and sit on the seat. We didn't have YouTube for quick lessons and the guys in the bicycle shop had no idea how to ride the strange wheel.

"What do you think?" I asked Steve.

"I'm not sure. As the pedals rotate, the balance point under the seat changes."

"Right. No coasting and braking like a bicycle. The pedal turns the wheel forward and backward." I put the wheel next to the wall and tried to step up onto a pedal and seat at the same time. Stepping on the pedal pushed the other pedal up and backward to smack into my shin as the seat moved forward. Down I fell, cursing and rolling on the ground as Steve laughed.

"That looked like it really hurt," he said.

"Shut up. You try to get on."

Steve cautiously repeated my performance and was shortly rolling on the ground with a bruised shin also. We both burst out laughing.

"This isn't going to be easy," he said.

"Maybe not, but I can learn anything."

That first afternoon we spent a lot of time smashing our legs and scraping our hands on the driveway as we fell over and over. Cutoff jeans were mandatory attire in the summer heat, leaving the knees exposed to coarse pavement. We quit beating ourselves up at dinner time and vowed to learn to ride my new toy.

The next afternoon, I told Steve, "I'm going to hold onto the wall with one hand and you hold onto my other hand to keep me up."

"That might work."

I positioned one pedal all the way down and held onto the seat as I stepped up. The seat came under me and I reached out for Steve. He grabbed my hand to stabilize me. I stayed up.

"That's the trick," I said as the seat and wheel moved back and forth independently. "Okay, now I'll pedal." The problem was, the top pedal didn't turn the way I wanted, so it went backward as I leaned forward and fell into Steve's arms.

"I don't think that's the trick," he said.

"Damn. Let me do it again." Over and over I tried, but I couldn't control the top pedal.

"My turn," Steve finally said.

Same story. He kept tumbling down on me as the wheel went where it wanted to go independently of the seat. After a couple of hours of beating ourselves up, we were worn out and dripping with sweat.

"Steve, this is harder than the trampoline. But I'm not quitting. If those clowns can ride it so can I."

"Me too. We have to learn to ride this summer so Coach will let us use it in the shows."

"Right."

So began a long odyssey. For two or three hours a day in the scorching Texas sun, Steve and I tore up the unicycle seat from crashes and shredded our hands, knees, and shins. Good thing we were gymnasts and knew how to roll out of the falls without breaking ourselves. Still, we contributed much skin to hot asphalt that summer. Falling onto grass would have been much better, but there was no way to ride on lumpy grass. The day I learned to walk off the pedals and catch the seat with my hands without falling down was special. I gradually learned that the starting position should be with both pedals horizontal so I could control frontward and backward wheel turn. On a bicycle, I would sit straight up and pedal forward. I had to unlearn that bad habit and lean forward into a fall and then pedal the wheel up under the fall. Keep leaning and pedaling into a fall. It was particularly difficult to try to pedal in one direction and the darned wheel, for no good reason, would spin 360 degrees in any direction away from the direction the seat was going. I would flail my arms in all directions to control the balance and keep the seat over the top of the tire.

Once I conquered a semi-straight line, the next challenge was turning in a desired direction. I learned to throw my arm around my body in the direction of turn like when twisting on the trampoline. We gradually became smooth riders and could idle, which was stopping the unicycle in place and rock back and forth. I challenged Steve to ride up a street curb one day and in no time he figured out that his approach had to be adjusted so that the curb was hit with the right side pedal just past the top. Stepping hard on that top pedal and lifting on the seat scooted him up and over the curb. I had no choice but to learn also. I finally found a trick Steve could not copy when I started riding backward.

By the end of the summer, we had unicycle riding down pat. I told Coach we had a new act and I gave him a demonstration. He loved it and added it to the show. That is how I ended up riding my unicycle around the track of the Cotton Bowl as the Dallas Cowboys played the New York Jets in a preseason game. The best part was riding by Broadway Joe Namath as he warmed up. He looked over at me and grinned. I rode around the track until it was time for our act. We dragged the trampoline and mats to the middle of the field and performed acrobatics until game time. That does not happen anymore.

Once I entered college at the University of Texas, I rode around campus and fit in with the other crazy people of my 70's generation. After college, the unicycle hung on the garage wall until my daughter, Stephanie, was born. I started riding again to entertain her and hoped she would develop an interest in riding the one wheeled monster. To stimulate her curiosity, I would sit her on my shoulders as I rode around the street on the unicycle. Stephanie was fearless and I never fell with her on top. Sadly, she tried but never learned to ride my clown toy.

When I finally grew up in my 40's, the unicycle seldom left the garage. On occasion, I would step out on it just to prove to myself that I still had balance.

At age 61, I had major heart surgeries, knee replacements, concussions, and other ailments of old age. I lost my balance and quit trying to ride. When I told Stephanie I was selling my antique unicycle, she said no; that I could find my balance again. I laughed and forgot about it.

On January 1, 2019, I made a New Years resolution that I would learn to ride again. I dusted off the old seat and started over. Naturally, I crashed several times and was glad I could still roll with a fall. Now, two weeks later, I ride across the parking lot every day and am struggling to learn to turn again. This will be my way to get my muscles and heart strong again and keep my balance for many years to come.

THE END

THE FREEKIN FREAK

By Kevin Hughes

"Coach, you can't be serious. Are you really going to start a guy who never played a single snap of football - ever."

"Yes, Tom, I am. I knew him in High School. He can play. He just chose not to. You will see."

"Coach, no offense, but the Owner of the Team has already publicly stated that he thinks- let me get this quote correct:" I gave the Coach full power over the roster. I think he went nuts. He gets to give that kid three weeks. If that kid is a bust in three weeks, then both him and Coach will get their pink slips on the same day. Three weeks. That is all I have given him. Don't ask me again, I think it as stupid as you do. It is the Coach's team, I only own it."

The Coach merely smiled.

"That sounds like Mr. Sabbati. And I won't need to worry about my job after week three."

Tom shook his head. So did the other twenty members of the Press Corps. The Season opener is tomorrow and this new kid has still never taken a snap. Nobody can believe the Coach is even going to suit him up, let alone play. Not one snap in the preseason. Not one. And the kid is going to start?

Mr. Sabatti might be right. Coach has gone nuts.

*****

The big kid came over Coach's house about eight PM. As was usual for the big kid, he knocked quietly, and stood patiently. He never looked like he was in a hurry, or rushed, or pressed for time- even when he was. He thought about things before hand, so when he acted - it was with no hesitation or indecisiveness. It is what had made him one of the greatest Piano Prodigies of all time. If not the Greatest Period.

The Coach opened the door with a smile almost as wide as the big kid was tall.

"I see you got here in time. Come on in. Did you memorize the playbook like I asked?"

"Yes, Coach. I have a few questions about coverage. I looked at the films you gave me, and need to know if they will use man to man, or zone on me."

"Well I think they will use man to man, until they see how fast you are. Then they will use zone to cover. Then, well, I think they will try to be physical with you- double teams, and hits as you break off the line. It won't really matter. They don't know what you can do. Just have fun."

The big kid smiled as the Coach closed the door. They both walked to the film room in the basement. "Just have fun." The big kid liked the sound of that.

*****

The Coach was in his last year as a High School Football Coach. He had taken his team to the State finals seven out of the last nine years. He had won the State Championship five of those years. Now he was off to be the New Head Coach at State College after this final year as a HS Coach.

When the big kid was a Sophomore, the Coach saw him for the first time. Not at Football Practice, but in the Music Room. The Coach was walking to his Office when he heard the most amazing Piano Playing he had ever heard. Music ran in the Coach's Family. His mother was the Church Organist, his Father was a rather brilliant amateur Saxophone player. His brother Chris was First Chair Cello player with the LA Symphony; Coach himself could hold his own on the Acoustic Guitar. His sister was the lead vocalist at church, and had put out a couple of albums before she settled down to be a Mom.

It was rumored that both his Grandfather and Grandmother played during the War with Count Basie- until they produced a child for every year of that decade and couldn't travel anymore. Music of all kinds had filled the Coach's childhood just as much as Athletics had. His sister was an all state basketball player, his brother Chris was a State Champ Wrester (126 pounds). Coach, of course, had chosen baseball and football as his sports. By college Coach had decided that football was his ticket.

It was. Until...

"Boom!" One hit. A broken hip. And a career in the NFL over in the first pre-season game. Back to Ohio he went, with a limp and a better understanding of the game of Football. He started Coaching at his Alma Matter that very year.

So when Coach heard that incredible control, fine pitch, the emotion focused into each note, he went to the Music room to see who it was, or if it was a CD by one of the Masters. It was neither.

The person at the piano was huge. Even sitting down he dominated the room. Coach could see how broad his shoulders were. How those giant hands caressed notes out of that bang upped piano, giving the piano delusions of grandeur, as if it were a Steinway at Carnegie Hall, and not a beat up standard piano in a High school in Ohio. The music was pouring out of the kid, through his hands, and out into any ear that accepts beauty and perfection as a matched pair.

The room was full with about a dozen students, twenty teachers, and a few Janitors. All just listening. When the big kid stopped playing- no one clapped. They just bowed. The big kid turned beat red- whispered: "Thanks," and closed the keyboard. Then he stood up.

Coach whistled… silently to himself. The big kid had to be Six foot six or seven. He must have weighed 265 pounds or more…and if he had more than three percent body fat, Coach would give you the pink slip to his 1963 Camaro. 'I am going to win every game with that kid playing.' Was his first thought. He was wrong.

*****

The big kid did not want to play football. He told the Coach that. He did like to run though. If the Coach wanted him to come out for track in the Spring…he would. Coach explained that by then he would be coaching the State College.

"Why won't you play football?"

"I don't want to hurt my hands. And I am not done growing. I think."

"Why are you worried about your hands?"

"You heard me play. I need them to be in good shape to make my dream of being a Concert Pianist come true. I read that you shouldn't play football until your joints are fully formed. The Doctors tell me that will be when I am 21 years old.

So I can run track, and will - for fun. But no contact sports until I am old enough."

And that was that. Coach forgot all about the big kid, until his former assistant football Coach, who was the HS track Coach, called him in April.

*****

"Hey Coach. You remember that big kid that turned you down for Football in the Fall?"

"Oh, yeah. The Piano Player. What about him?"

"Well…I am going to send you a tape of him running."

"Why?"

"Because he just ran his first track meet for us. He won the Mile…and the 100 Meters."

Coach whistled at that. Nobody since Jim Thorpe (that Coach new of) had ever recorded that double in track.

"Wow!"

"Oh, don't "Wow" yet. There is more."

Coach laughed into the phone:

"What did he win the High Jump too?"

"No. But he probably could (that sobered the Coach's humor right up). What he did do was break the State record in the Mile run AND he ran the fastest 100 meter in High School History."

"That is impressive, but our High School was never noted for sprinters."

"No Coach. Not our High School record. The United States High School Record."

Coach almost dropped the phone, but managed to choke out a short:

"You don't say."

******

The next time Coach heard about the big kid, was five years later. Coach had won two National Championships at State College and narrowly missed a third. The NFL was sniffing around at the end of every season now. "Come Coach in the Big Leagues" was the siren call that seduced every coach worth his salt. And Coach had plenty of salt. So he did.

But he promised his wife a month of no Football. None. In fact, she wanted a month to herself with just Coach - and no Football buddies, players, or owners. The Coach put it in writing. He would start Coaching in the NFL, after a six week vacation. Coach smiled when he showed his wife the tickets to the Mediterranean. Two weeks onboard a luxury Cruise Ship and then they would pick which city to stay in for the rest of the time.

Even though it wasn't on the ship's itinerary, they chose Paris. It was as Romantic as they thought it would be. His wife grew up with a concert Pianist as one of her Brother's, and her Mom was a famous Opera Singer- so when they heard there was a special recital by a young phenom from America, they bought tickets.

When the lights went down, and the Pianist came out on stage, there was an audible gasp from the crowd. Coach almost choked. It was the big kid. And he was bigger. He must be six foot eight and 300 pounds…or more, thought the Coach, and I would still bet he doesn't have three percent body fat. (And the Coach was right)

After words, the reviewers and reviews reflected just how good the big kid really was. Critics are hard to please, these Critics must have been from a different breed, because they fought over finding adjectives that would convey the intense feeling the big kid created with his music. One even said in print:

"If keys produced color instead of sound, there would be yellows that blind the eyes, reds that drip wine and blood into your soul, and raging electric blues that arouse even the most indifferent ear."

And that was understatement.

Coach and his wife smuggled themselves past the gatekeepers by using the simple tactic of stating that they taught at the High School the big kid learned to play at. The Publicist recognized the name of the High School, checked with the big kid, and agreed to let them come back stage.

For five nights in a row, Coach and his wife went to the Sold Out concerts. During the day they went sightseeing with the big kid in tow. At night, after the concerts, they went to dinner together.

"Come play football for me."

The big kid would smile every time the Coach asked him.

"When I retire from my Concert Playing Days."

"Ok. When will that be?"

"As soon as they don't want me anymore."

*****

The big kid was only 21 years old when it happened. His recordings would last forever. But the big kid had played his last concert. It was one of those things nobody could have predicted. It was an accident. A cruel one. In one of the most beautiful cities in the world: Venice, Italy. The gondola he was riding in was swamped by a drunk rich Venetian with too much money and no sense. As the motor boat sped by, the wake pushed his gondola up against the brick of a villa. Unfortunately, he was holding the gondolas gunwale with his left hand.

That moment altered his life, ended his career, and changed his plans. The Doctors were good, the Surgeons even better. The big kid's hand and thumb had been broken in thirteen places. They put it together again, but he would never play the piano again. His hand worked for ordinary things like holding a cup, or catching a ball, but not for the fine motor control to play at the Maestro level.

So he called Coach.

******

The Phone rang. Coach picked it up not recognizing the number, but he knew the voice as soon as he heard it speak:

"Coach, I am retired now. Do you want me to come play?"

"Yes."

*****

"Nothing that big should be that fast. Nothing that fast should be that big."

That was the Headline of the biggest newspaper in the State. The big kid had changed the game. Six foot eight inches tall, weighing three hundred twenty pounds, with a sixty inch chest and a thirty two inch waist and the speed of an Olympic Sprinter. He played his first game as a wide receiver.

The stats speak for themselves, and will echo down the generations of Football Fans forever:

Catches: 14

Yards: 1,084

Touchdowns: 11

One game.

*****

Mister Sabatti promptly signed both the big kid and the Coach to long term contracts. The week three deadline was ignored. If not forgotten.

Tom spoke up at the Press Conference:

"Coach, I called you nuts. I am sorry. How did you know he could do that?"

Before Coach could answer, the big kid stood up and went to the podium.

"I told him I could. I like to run, and he told me if I could catch - it would work out fine. It did." And that laughter drowned out most of the next ten minutes until the Quarter Back (who had just thrown for a NFL record One thousand, one hundred and six yards) said (when asked what he thought of the big kid's play):

"He's a Freekin Freak."

The name stuck.

THE END

THE LAST BOAT RIDE

By Gordon England

My phone rang on Thursday night. Good, I'd been waiting. Kristian Kwiecinski's name showed on the caller ID.

"Hey buddy," I said. "Give me a good report."

"I just came back from the Nassau docks and tuna were being cleaned."

"Blackfin or skipjacks?"

"Both. The usual school of skippies is off the west end of the island, but blackfins have been schooling off the north side this week."

"What time of the day?"

"They were hitting late this afternoon."

"Great. This is the first time in a month there've been blackfins at the docks. These doldrums will keep the sea flat until a hurricane wanders our way. Nobody will be in the office tomorrow afternoon, so come on over around five and we'll make a quick run."

"Sounds good. I'll see you then."

I went outside to my driveway where Boat Tales, my 21-foot Aquasport, waited for me to finish loading fishing gear in her cabin. I prepared an array of tuna jigs for fast trolling on Penn rods and gold reels. No dead ballyhoo for bait tomorrow; they would spin and shred when trolled above eight knots. While yellowfin tuna grew to a hundred pounds or more, the smaller backfins were typically under twenty pounds. Though a resident school of lowly skipjack tuna stayed north of the island in the afternoons, their dark meat was too bloody for my taste. Back in Florida, blackfins had dark meat also, but their diet in the Bahamas was a different kind of baitfish that turned their flesh white, almost as good as the yellowfins I caught on long runs to the Abacos or Andros. A fisherman's network at the docks let when to make a close run for the blackfins.

I had Boat Tales' trailer hooked up when Kristian showed up with ice. He was a thirtyish, white Panamanian, short and stout with short dark hair and brusque face. Strong arms and back served him well for chasing large tuna and billfish. We both sported full-length UV protected shirts, long-billed hats, and polarized sunglasses to better see the fish. I also wore thin fishing gloves to protect my hands from the sun and perilous items encountered aboard a bouncing boat.

"Glad to see you out of that coat and tie," I said while putting ice in the fish box.

He smiled. "I gotta do what I gotta do."

His day job was an international banker, one of the few Bahamian businessmen who dressed in a suit. His only clients were rich businessmen from Mexico and Central America with accounts of $1,000,000 or more. They hid their money in the Bahamas so that their local banks would not watch their accounts to find kidnapping targets. Like the movie Man on Fire. He was also a tournament fisherman and regular first mate on Boat Tales.

I drove to the gates at the private port of Sandyport on the west end of Cable Beach, and with a bored face, flashed my government ID. When the guard waved me through, I proceeded to the sole boat ramp on the north side of the island and launched the boat. We waited for the guard under the Bay Street bridge to lower a cable at the end of the channel. He reminded us that he would lock the cable and leave at nine o'clock, closing the port until the next morning. When my boat tower cleared the bridge, I pushed the throttle forward. Boat Tales rose to a plane as we cleared the jetty, her deep bow sliced through the Bahamian Sea. I steered a northerly course toward the fishing grounds ten miles in the distance. The brilliant yellow sun threw hot rays across an empty blue sky, glittering on the rippled water to the west of us, and revealing clear aquamarine water to the east. A mile offshore, the water turned cobalt blue when we left Nassau's reef and entered the 2,000-foot deep Tongue of the Ocean. The heavy salt air cleared my mind, pushing away stress and aggravation as I ran away to a world of wind, sun, and water.

"Good thing you have banker's hours and left work early," I said.

"Hey, even the bank is on island time."

"How's your wife doing?"

"She's due in two weeks."

"This will be your last fishing run for a while."

"Afraid so. I'll be losing sleep for a few months."

"Are you going to keep fishing the tournaments next year?"

"Of course. That's not going to stop."

"I didn't get a report from you about the IGFA World Championship. I take it you didn't win."

He shook his head with a grimace. "That was in Cabo San Lucas again. We caught three marlins on the first two days and were in the running for first place. On the last day, I caught one at 156 pounds, but another team from Cape Hatteras landed a 302 pounder and won the tournament."

"Soo close. What kind of marlin did you catch?"

"They were all stripers. Blues and blacks come later in the summer."

"I bet there were good parties over there in Mexico," I teased with a smile.

"Not beforehand, we were getting ready. But afterward, oh yeah." He laughed. "Lots of tequila."

"What did the trip cost you?"

"The entry fee was $10,000 for the team. We booked a boat for a week and went there a few days early to learn the waters. Then we had tips for first mates and hotels. It added up."

"And betting in the Calcutta?"

Boat captains had their own side bets in a fishing pool.

"Of course." He gave me a sly look. "We made enough on that to pay the entry fee."

"You're running with the big boys."

"Oh yeah."

I turned the wheel over to Kristian and prepared four rods, two with medium sized cedar plugs and two with high speed skirted hooks on monofilament leaders. I didn't use wire leader that tended to kink at high speed, because tuna didn't have sharp teeth like other large fish. We put on fishing belts with cups to keep rod butts from bruising our stomachs. It was time to hunt. I climbed to my lookout perch in the tower as Kristian zigzagged northward. I looked back to see New Providence Island recede into the blueness as afternoon storm clouds built over her warm land. We were on our own with Mother Ocean and her bounty.

***

Yes, living in the Bahamas had turned into an incredible adventure. My wife, Annie, and I had moved to Nassau two years ago when I landed a job as the Drainage Engineer for the government's Ministry of Works. Normally, jobs for non-Bahamians were difficult to find unless they needed specialized skills. I became the first U.S. engineer hired by the Bahamian government because of my expertise with stormwater flooding and pollution control. I happened to place an inquiry for a job opening at the right time. When the offer came, we ridded ourselves of many of our worldly trappings, packed light, and moved to the Bahamas, me in Boat Tales and Annie by plane with our cat, Luci Belle. Being a fanatic deep sea fisherman, combined with an insatiable desire to explore Jimmy Buffet's magical islands, I quickly vanished into paradise. For me, this was the best of both worlds. The Ministry welcomed my engineering forte as I rapidly addressed multitudes of flooding issues, small and large, across the many islands. Management gave me a free hand to see what I could accomplish. Whenever I requested project funding, I watched the Minister of Works take the paperwork through Parliament and bring back an approval in short order. They were pleased to have someone making improvements to their islands. The Bahamian people were friendly and open to my suggestions for reorganizing staff duties, hiring contractors, giving news interviews for projects, and designing one of the first large retention ponds for flood control in the Bahamas. I was back to the basics of surveying, engineering, and construction with no pesky permits, regulators, and oversight that made work difficult in the States. Along with the professional satisfaction of improving the infrastructure in the Bahamas, Annie and I escaped on many weekends on Boat Tales to explore hidden harbors, catch multitudes of large fish, dive on rainbow reefs, and raise a toast to Margaritaville.

***

Thirty minutes later, we closed in on a smudge on the horizon which became specks of birds. I climbed down the ladder and pointed. Kristian maintained twenty-five knots as he turned toward the flock. He slowed to watch the swirling birds dive into splashing water that boiled with baitfish driven to the surface by a swarm of flashing tuna.

"They're headed east," he said and sped up to circle in front of the fast-moving school of tuna.

I grabbed a rod, released the drag, and dropped a cedar plug. It hit the water and spun line off the reel until I tightened the drag at thirty yards. I lowered the rod into an outside holder and set two more lures at forty yards and the shotgun line back at sixty yards. Kristian turned the boat, timing our speed so that the lures crossed the leading edge of birds and fish. A starboard rod bent, the reel screaming sweet music. I pulled the rod from the holder and cranked the reel. No need to set the hook. The tuna had hooked himself when it hit the lure at high speed. Kristian slowed the boat to ease my fight and reeled in the other lures. After two short runs, I brought the fish aboard and dropped it in the fish box. Kristian slammed the lid on the furious tuna. It's tail fluttered hard against fiberglass for several minutes before giving up the fight. Tuna are one of the toughest of all fish.

"Way to go, Gordon."

"First fish," I replied, high-fiving Kristian. "Your position was perfect with the boat."

"Always."

"You're probably a better first mate than banker."

"I just wish it paid as good."

I pointed at the same flock ahead of us. "They're still up; let's go. I'll drive. It's your turn to fish."

I took the wheel and sped after the fast-moving school. Boat Tales was running at twenty knots before I gained on the birds. When I moved alongside the swarm, the water went quiet before Kristian dropped lures. The tuna had sounded into deep water.

"The fish are spooky this time of the year after being chased all summer," he said.

"Yes, we'll be lucky to get more than one pass at a school."

The tuna bird flock dissipated, and the sea was still. I turned north again in search of more fish. Ten minutes later, Kristian pointed west at a few birds. I turned, and the birds became a flock diving into boiling water. He set the lures out as I crossed ahead of the melee. I slowed a bit to drop the lures beneath the surface. Kristian stood between the rods, ready to grab any of them. I waited with anticipation as fish splashed around the lines. Any time now. One reel spun in protest.

"Fish on," yelled Kristian.

The line veered to the starboard side. Good. It wouldn't tangle the other lines. He picked up the rod, spread his legs for balance, and cranked. I turned the wheel to port, away from the tuna and slipped the engine into neutral. We slowed, and the swarm of birds and fish engulfed us in chaos. Another rod dipped.

"Better get that one, Gordon."

I picked it up, pushed the drag all the way tight, and turned the reel. The line approached the boat as the tuna dove deep. I reached back with one hand and bumped the engine into gear to stay ahead of the fish, then put the rod back in the holder so I could help Kristian.

"How are you doing over there?" I asked.

"It's not too big, maybe 10 pounds. I'll have him in soon."

"Do you need a gaff?"

"Maybe not."

I snatched the gaff from a tower rod holder just in case. A glance at my line showed my fish was almost under the engine as it struggled to follow the school ahead of us. I pushed the throttle forward a little more and turned the wheel gently. No need to throw Kristian off balance. His blackfin was at the gunwale now, not too big but still putting up a good fight.

"Don't need a gaff," he said. I opened the fish box and stepped back. He dropped his rod tip to the stern, stepped into the corner of the deck against the transom, and reeled the line all the way tight against the leader. With a shoveling motion, he heaved the fish out of the water, twisted, and dropped a beautiful backfin into the box.

I shut the lid as the tuna dance began. Rattle rattle rattle.

"Way to go," I cheered with a high five.

"Your turn."

I took my rod and brought in another medium sized fish for our first double-header of the day.

We continued chasing bird flocks and bringing in more fish for another hour. By now we were fifteen miles from home.

"The fish gods have been good to us," I said. "Let's head home and save some for next time."

"Okay, but we might see more on the way back."

"You never know."

I throttled up with reluctance and took a wide turn, putting the sun to my right. Staying out until dark would be fun but I did not want to spend the night at the port gate. Kristian climbed the ladder and took the lookout bench. I weaved in long, gentle turns on the smooth blue water. Halfway back to Sandyport, Kristian interrupted my tropical thoughts.

"Birds at two o'clock."

He descended to the deck as I steered toward a blur in the sky that soon turned into a swarm of birds. A few minutes later, we cautiously approached the thrashing multitudes of bait and fish. I stayed fifty yards away to keep from spooking them.

"Which way are they swimming?" I asked.

"Straight into the sun."

I took a course to run around the birds while Kristian let out the lures.

"The fish look a little different," I noted.

"Yes. Not as many, but bigger than the others we've been catching."

"The bigger the better."

"I'll drive. It's your turn to catch one."

I turned over the wheel and tightened my fish belt. I checked the drags on the reels. Too loose and the line would slip out. Too tight and the hooks would rip out of the fish's mouth when it struck. Everything was ready. Kristian pulled ahead of the school, then slowed down. I watched the lures as noisy water and birds approached. A big tuna leaped out of the water in a perfect arch and savagely attacked the shotgun cedar plug, landing with an enormous splash. A rod bowed, its reel singing a high-pitched song.

"Fish on," I shrieked. "It's the biggest tuna I've ever seen."

Kristian slowed down and replied, "It's too big to be a blackfin. Must be a yellowfin. Hang on to him." He brought in the other lures and cleared the deck of rods, buckets, and gaffs in anticipation of a major struggle.

I planted the butt of the rod into my fish belt, tightened the drag, and watched the reel spin. And spin. No use reeling until this first run ended. A hundred yards out it finally stopped.

"Kristian. Give me a hand and chase him. I don't want to fight all night."

He turned the boat and sped toward the fish. I pumped and reeled, pumped and reeled, inching back line. This tuna was powerful. When the fish sensed the nearing boat, it dove. Deep and hard. Kristian steered until my line was nearly straight down, but still swimming at a good pace.

"Keep reeling," he commanded.

"Yeah, yeah." I bent my knees and rocked back as hard as I could to lift the rod. Then dropped the tip and reeled to gain a couple of feet of line. Over and over.

"You're right," I said through gritted teeth. "Gotta be a yellowfin. This will be my first."

"Tighten the drag."

I pushed the lever a little more. Pump and reel. For every six inches I gained, I lost two. What a test of strength. Me versus the fish. Pump and reel for fifteen minutes. I stopped to rest.

"This is your fish, Gordon. If you let it rest, it'll win. Keep on reeling."

Grrr. Back to cranking.

This would be my biggest tuna. Maybe even bigger than my 105-pound sailfish from Panama.

Kristian kept the boat directly over the fish as I slowly brought line onto the reel. "Keep pumping," he yelled.

I was in a zone, totally focused on the fish and putting line back on the reel. And the pain in my arms and back.

"I can see color," Kristian exclaimed. "You're almost there."

I saw the tuna at the same time it saw the boat. Line buzzed off the reel again. A second run started to the bottom. Back down a hundred feet. Oh God, not again. Time to start over. I tightened the drag to full stop and heaved up again. Wound down. Halfway into the next lift, the line went limp. No! Was it coming to the surface? I reeled furiously. Nothing. My shoulders slumped.

"What happened?" asked Kristian.

"It's gone." I slowly wound in the line. The intact lure cleared the water. I grabbed it and looked at the hook. Uhn.

"I used medium hooks for the little blackfin. He straightened it." I shook my head in misery.

Kristian grimaced. "You fought it well. Next time you'll get him."

"The one that got away. Let's call it a day."

I was disappointed about losing a big fish, but the day had been great.

We secured the gear, opened two Kalik beers, and tapped their tops together. I brought Boat Tales up to cruising speed on a southerly bearing. The low orange sun shimmered on dead flat water hissing against Boat Tales hull as she skated back to port. I thought about today's story. Part of Mother Ocean's magic was that no two voyages were the same. She revealed something memorable on each trip.

"You handled yourself pretty good today," Kristian said.

"Yeah, it was fun."

"You know, our fishing team has gone to the World Championship Tournament the last couple of years. One of the guys dropped out. Would you like to join the team and fish with us at Cabo San Lucas?" He grinned, knowing what was going through my mind.

I paused for a moment, thinking about the ultimate fishing trip. "I'm really honored, Kristian. I know there would be several qualifying tournaments over the next year as well. I'm afraid that's out of my league. Government bureaucrats don't make banker's money. I wish I could."

"Okay. Just thought I'd ask." We clinked beers again.

"Take the wheel. I'm going up top."

I climbed the tower and stood in front of the bench with my arms out and hat off. Salty wind fluttered through my clothes. The engine hummed. A perfectly round orange sun touched the sea just beyond my reach as I floated through the air. The horizon encircled me with an eternal blue line. There would not be a more perfect day on a more glorious sea for the rest of my life. My job was wonderful, my wife was great, and the islands spun their magic on me. What more could I want?

Little did I know that the world would take a left turn and that would be my last ride on Boat Tales. Islanders have a saying that sooner or later we all end up in the soup, and I did. But that is another story.

THE END

SURPRISE LANDING

By Gordon England

In far west Texas, Big Bend National Park along the Rio Grande River is the state's crown jewel, bigger than Rhode Island. This northern edge of Mexico's Chihuahuan desert offers an astounding collage of rugged mountains, desert with scattered scrub and cactus, and winding waters of the Rio Grande River that created and mystic allure that called to me for an outdoors vacation with my wife Susan in the summer of 1983.

After a ten-hour high-speed drive across Texas from San Antonio to Big Bend, we reached Terlingua at the west side of the Chisos Mountains, just a short hop to the Rio Grande River. I say high-speed drive because the roads are long straight runs across the desert where a police car can be seen ten miles in any direction. With vast distances to traverse, I pushed the pedal to a speed that did not quite overheat the engine.

Terlingua has a storied history, once known as the Quicksilver Capital of the World where 2,000 miners eked out a harsh existence in the rocky desert. The mine closed after World War II, leaving a ghost town in the National Park until 1967 when Frank Tolbert and Wick Fowler held the World Chili Championship and brought the town back to life as a popular tourist attraction in desolate West Texas. Many musical events and cookouts have sprung from those early days. Though the permanent population is now only a few dozen, restaurants and hotels cater to year-round tourism with the biggest attraction being an old jail.

We checked into a rustic motel in a valley surrounded by ragged mounts and hidden mines. At the saloon, we ate an obligatory steak dinner with beer, listened to cowboy music, and spent a little time in the jail listening to ghosts of the past. Shadows crept upon us as rugged peaks swallowed the sun. We climbed a hill to watch multitudes of stars twinkle close enough to grab while we listened to complete silence.

The next morning, we met our two rafting guides, Jim and Tony, from Far Flung Adventures and ten other adventurers in Lajitas, a village alongside the Rio Grande. The primary entertainment consisted of watching the mayor, a goat named Clay Henry III, grab a bottle of beer and raise it high to guzzle bubbling brew. The desert does strange things to people. And goats. Across the river in the village of Boquillas, Mexico (though still in the National Park) Mexicans gathered on the water's edge to waded through a rare shallow water crossing to meet with relatives and buy supplies on the US side.

Our guides loaded waterproof bags held food, tents, and supplies on two ten-foot rafts. They explained the three-day journey through Santa Elena Canyon of the Rio Grande Gorge with many Class II and III rapids. We were lucky the high water level at 1,250 feet per second meant no portaging around brutal Class IV rapids of the Rockslide Rapids at the end of the Gorge. Once we entered Santa Elena, the only escape would be by raft. The canyons were too narrow for helicopter rescues.

Every person in the rafts would row with oars in oarlocks on this working vacation. Jim and Tony sat in the rear to issue commands and steer while the others stroked. A previous trip on this river convinced me that bringing my own kayak to navigate the Rio Grande would be a fun challenge. I blew up the yellow, twelve-foot inflatable vessel and launched behind the rafts. We pushed away from shore and entered a bleak landscape of sand, rocks, and the hundred-foot-wide river slicing through mountains. All in countless shades of tan. Susan and I initially rode the kayak together in the slow current of this first stretch of Mesquite and scrub-lined shoreline. The temperature rapidly rose to 100 degrees as the sun swung overhead. I settled into a relaxed rhythm of listening to the voice of the water while dipping my double-ended paddle just enough to steer straight behind the rafts. The river never fell to complete silence; a quiet whisper meant deep and slow while splashing warned of shallow and fast.

We drifted through small hills and flatlands that first morning, getting the feel for the river. I paddled while Susan lay back in the front seat and soaked up sun and silence. We stayed behind the rafts, following them through shallow water and around occasional boulders. The guides served sandwiches for lunch on a sandbar. I liked this no cooking vacation. The other rafters quizzed me about my kayak, a relatively new type of craft. I pointed out that the draft was less than a canoe and the hollow compartments absorbed boulder blows without knocking me overboard.

Later that afternoon, the massive brown mountains of Santa Elena Canyon rose higher and the river's rustle grew louder we approached. The water's speed increased as the width narrowed. We stopped to camp on the last sandbar before entering the canyon that now roared at us in defiance.

"This is as far as we go today," a Jim informed us and pointed. "One-day trips end here and leave by a road over that hill. We'll camp here tonight and enter Santa Elena in the morning. If anyone wants to back out, this is your last chance." He paused, but no one spoke up. "Once we're in we have to go all the way. By the way, rockslides frequently change the course and we don't know how to get through them until we get there."

While I looked in silence, the water's roar echoed off the imposing walls of Santa Elena's cliffs. Many thoughts went through my head and surely the others too. How did the river cut fifteen hundred feet straight up one rock? How bad were the rapids? Frequent rock slides? Where would we camp the next night? And most importantly, could I successfully traverse the Gorge without smashing myself on the rocks. This is what we had signed up for, but there were no words on paper that could have prepared me for this freaky canyon of nature.

Susan said, "Good luck. I'll be on a raft tomorrow."

"Yes, you are. Don't worry. I can do this," I said with false bravado.

The guides set up camp and lit a gas stove to cook dinner. No use looking for firewood in the desert. As the sun set across the mountains, we ate delicious steaks, salads, veggies, and a Dutch oven apple pie. After dinner, the guides entertained us with stories of explorers and Indians from yesteryear in West Texas.

The next morning, we received a lecture from Jim. "This is what you signed up for. Lots of rapids, so keep your life jackets on and buckled at all times. Stay in your own place on the rafts and listen for our commands for rowing. If we run into a rock, don't try to push away on it. You'll just get thrown into the water and we'll have to divert to save you. If the raft flips, hang onto it and we'll get it turned over. If you fall out, don't try to swim through the rapids. Your face will get smashed on a rock. Put your feet together in front of you and lean back. Let your feet and butt hit the rocks. Once you're through a rapid, swim to a calm spot and wait for us to pick you up. Any questions?"

"Has anybody been hurt before?" someone asked.

"Yes, but mostly sprains and bruises. By the way, Gordon, have you kayaked in Class III rapids before?"

"No, just smaller rivers in the Hill Country."

"It gets pretty hairy in places. If you want help, I'll ride with you on the bigger rapids."

"It wasn't too bad last year on the raft. If I change my mind, I'll let you know." The enormous rock wall at the entrance to the gorge in front of us stared in disdain . Turbulent water hid any apparent twist or turn; the river seemed to just disappear into chaos.

"Which way is the first turn?" I asked.

He laughed. "A sharp left. Stay close to us so I can keep an eye on you."

"Let's go," I said, building up courage.

We packed our gear, buckled life jackets, and stepped into our respective vessels of fun for day number two. I waited for the rafts to leave first, then pushed off into fast water. The guides knew the safe routes through these canyon waters, which made my job a lot easier. I steered the light craft using moderate strokes to follow about twenty yards behind the second raft. As I approached the thundering entrance, the raft in front of me spun to the left and accelerated down a narrow, fast chute. No time for fear as tunnel vision took over. Smooth water was safe. Whitewater frothing over rocks meant danger. I dug deep with my trailing left oar for a left turn and dropped down splashing rapids cascading one after another. Losing control would allow the river to turn the kayak sideways and roll over. Ten seconds and a hundred yards later, I emerged from the Gorge's first run and paddled around a corner to the rafts where my companions cheered for me. Adrenalin rushed through my veins like I had been on a roller coaster. This would be a fun day.

After a couple of turns, the river's roar subsided to a whisper. We now floated through a land of tan water with parched, tan rock on both sides reaching virtually straight up a thousand feet toward a blue ribbon of sky. No vegetation, no wildlife, no blistering sun to burn us. Just the Rio Grande's world where she reigned over our miniscule boats, pushing us this way and that, from a whisper to a ro ar, from slow to fast. The foolish and unprepared could not survive. One mistake from me spelled disaster.

A low rumble gradually increased in volume. Jim looked at me and smiled. "Here we go again."

"I'm ready." I felt invincible.

"This one's not bad. Stay to the right."

Around the next bend, a roar started where a small rockslide had filled the gorge with scattered boulders. I stayed back to watch the rafts veer right and hug the perpendicular wall to avoid the treacherous riverbed. At lower water levels, we would have been portaging. One raft swirled in an eddy and ended up sideways to the current. That didn't look good, but they dug in hard and fast with their oars to straighten out as the Tony barked orders. With the path in mind, I began the run in the middle between two rocks and then cut right as thundering water splashed high on the left. Hard strokes brought me next to the wall. A push against it with my paddle straightened the kayak out. Light strokes kept my nimble craft centered in the current until the river spat me out into calm water again.

Our day continued in a series of rapids and still waters, thunder and quiet. Later that afternoon, our guides found a camping spot for the night on a small stretch of sand under a rock overhang. The narrow sandbar had room for tents and the air was stifling, so we unrolled our sleeping bags next to the water to sleep under to the stars. As we ate dinner and drank cold beer, I pointed up and asked Tony, "Is that a cave on the other side, a couple hundred feet up?"

"Yes," he replied and snuck a look at Jim. "There's a few caves in these mountains." He changed the subject and said, "Tomorrow we finish at Rockslide Rapids. At this water level, they're normally a Class IV run, which we can make. We leave Class V rapids to whitewater experts and nobody runs Class VI. When we get close to rocks, pull in the oars. Another guide told me last week that a recent rockslide changed our usual course, so we'll scout out a new route when we stop for lunch. If you don't want to do this, Gordon, I'll take your kayak through for you. It's been a while since I've run the Box alone."

"I'll let you know after we look at it." I left my options open. The rapids had been fun so far, but I wasn't feeling suicidal.

Darkness came early when the sun fell behind canyon walls.

Right at dusk, Susan pointed across the river and yelled, "What that?"

A cloud rolled out of the cave, swirling in an upward spiral.

"Bats," replied Jim.

Two other girls screamed as the rest of us laughed.

"Don't worry," said Tony. "They go up into the desert looking for bugs. There's no food down here for them."

We stared in awe for several minutes as thousands of bats flew impossibly close to each other from their cave. Their radar sensing ability was a wonder of nature.

After a hard day of paddling through rapids, sleep came easy, though Susan insisted on being inside her sleeping bag in case the bats came back. I slept under the stars on top of mine to catch a bit of coolness as the Rio Grande sang us to sleep.

Before pushing off the next morning, Jim warned us, "Today we step up to Class IV water at the Rockslide. Susan, you can ride with Gordon until we get there. Then you'll get back in the raft and Gordon will decide what he wants to do."

We drifted in total relaxation for a couple of hours through calm water and light rapids. I loved being away from the world to receive deep recharges from Mother Nature. No traffic, no phones, no stress in this land unchanged through the ages.

We rounded a bend and heard a familiar rumble. One more challenge lay ahead at Rockslide Rapids. Ahead of us, an enormous section of canyon wall had fallen into the river, scattering car and house-sized boulders for a mile downstream. The rafts stopped behind a fifty-foot high dam of boulders. I pulled my kayak onto a rock next to them. Susan transferred to a raft as the guides and I scrambled to the top of the dam and stared at a formidable sight below. Innumerable boulders lay strewn across the water hap hazardously as far as I could see. Shallow rapids were not the issue. Our challenge was to find a path through the maze without running into a dead end where fast water would crush us against rocks and suck us under.

"Do you know how to get through this mess?" I asked.

"I used to. Now there are new rocks so I'm not sure ," replied Jim.

For half an hour, we watched the river and tried to figure out a path. I looked back at the rafts and saw a lone canoe coming down the canyon.

"Let's watch him," I said.

Thank goodness the fellow in the canoe knew the safe route. We watched him successfully zigzag around and through the rockslide, emerging far downstream unscathed.

"Did you catch that path?" Jim asked.

"Yes," said Tony.

"Uh, I'm not sure I can maneuver it," I replied.

"Here's what we'll do," said Jim. "You stay here and watch us take the rafts through. I'll come back and ride with you in the kayak."

"Sounds good to me."

I watched from above as the valiant crews responded to their guide's commands to row hard left, right, and sideways through the series of narrow openings between boulders and appear intact at the end. I knew then I did not have the strength to paddle and radically turn through many small openings by myself. A second person paddling gave the necessary power to maneuver and stay alive on this run.

As I sat on the precipice, the river's thunder and power mesmerized me. The pounding would continue for thousands of years, grinding the boulders down to gravel and sand. I was just a blink to the Gorge today.

Soon the Jim returned and sat down to rest. He pointed out the route and special problems they encountered.

"Are you ready?" he shouted over the river noise.

"As ready as I'll ever be."

"Let's do this. We'll use single oars. Up front, your instinct to steer with a second bl ade will screw us up. I'll do the steering from the rear. You listen to my commands for which side to row on. We'll start in on the second entrance."

We returned to my kayak, climbed aboard, and pushed off for one last rapid. We crossed the river to the second opening in the wall and spun right into fast water through a narrow crack that the other rafts had barely squeezed through.

"Left," yelled Jim as we raced toward a pile of boulders.

I paddled on the left side while he held his blade down on the right. We turned into another gap and shot through in seconds. We careened back and forth through giant rocks and rapids as Jim shouted instructions to me at a pace that left no time for fear. Just total concentration on each stroke to avoid crashing and rolling. He expertly steered us on the right path until we reached a slow pool where the rafts awaited with our cheering comrades. We had made it through Rockslide Rapids. I stayed pumped for quite a while as Jim and Susan changed places for the smooth ride out of Santa Elena.

"I can't believe you made it," she said, shaking her head. "I screamed all the way through."

"I only made it because the guide knew the way." Fear crept in as adrenaline faded. "That's the last time I'm going on a Class IV."

A few miles later the canyon disgorged us back to silent stair stepped hills. We pulled into a staging point where other rafters were putting in for an extended trip through the highly dangerous Lower Canyons with many portages and Class IV rapids.

One of them asked me, "First time I've seen an inflatable kayak. How did it do in Rockslide?"

"No problem. It's actually lighter than a canoe so it turns faster and bounces off rocks."

"Cool."

"Have you been through the Lower Canyons before?"

"No, this is my first time. I had to sign a release form this morning. They get a lot of guys banged up down there."

"Be safe," I said in amazement. These guys were braver than I would ever be. I take that back. They weren't brave. They were crazy.

I said goodbye to the wondrous river and drove back to civilization at the hotel. Back at the saloon that night we enjoyed hearty steaks and beer again. This could be habit forming.

The next morning, we left the hotel for our next adventure. At nearby Lajitas International Airport, a small landing strip next to the border, we entered the small terminal building.

"Is this where we can take a sightseeing flight?" I asked the fellow at the desk.

"Sure is. Let me call the pilot." He picked up a microphone and said, "Frank, come in."

"Frank here."

"There's a couple of folks that want a flight. Are you available?"

"I'll be there shortly."

"10-4." He looked at me. "Frank's got the best sightseeing trip around here." He laughed. "As a matter of fact, he's the only one.

You'll like Frank. He's the County Sheriff. Only one of those out here too. We don't have much cause for a Sheriff around here. Except for drunk tourists. Now when they have that big chili cook-off in Terlingua, we have to bring in a few highway patrols to help out. Well here comes Frank now."

I looked out the window as a police car parked out front. A middle-aged, slightly balding man in blue jeans and tee shirt walked through the door. No police hat or gun. Things were pretty laid back out here in West Texas.

"Hello. I'm Frank." He held out his hand.

I shook it, noting a firm grip. "I'm Gordon England and this is my wife, Susan."

"Pleased to meet you. You lookin' for a tour around the mountains?"

"Yes, we are. What are your rates for the two of us?"

"How does half an hour for a hundred dollars sound?"

"Just right."

"Great. Let's get some paperwork filled out."

We signed our lives away and followed Frank out to an old four-seat Piper Cub.

As Frank went through his preflight check, Susan noted, "This is a really old plane." She had not been in a small plane before.

"Mm."

"Think it's safe?"

"I don't know, but as long as Frank does, we should be okay."

When Frank finished, we climbed into two seats behind him and he started the engine. He taxied to the runway and we took off. There were no tower or other planes to worry about. The Sheriff did what he wanted.

While Big Bend had dazzled us as we had driven around the bottom of the mountains, looking from above opened a whole new dimension of grandeur to this incredible landscape that could not be seen by car. The small Chisos Mountain Range lay entirely in the National park, rising 5,000 feet above the Rio Grande River. Stark browns, tans, and greys spread in every direction, with just an occasional patch of wicked green yucca spears. The lone highway in and out of the park gave the only indication of mankind. Frank flew low over Lajitas and along the river dividing two countries. He rose over Santa Elena Canyon and traced our rafting route on the silver thread far below. I had a hard time believing we had been way down there yesterday with the Gorge howling at us. Next, he flew over the mountain's high volcanic rims that fell into unpassable bottoms.

The vast landscape's spell on me broke when Frank's voice came over the headset, "Looks like we're getting low on gas. I need to refuel."

I looked at Susan and shrugged. Okay, we need gas. He turned on a course away from the airport. The plane descended toward the desert. I wondered where we're going. Lower and lower. Over a highway. Why were we over the two-lane highway?

"Uh, Frank. Where are we going for gas?" I asked.

"The gas station."

"You're landing on the highway?"

"Don't worry. I can see for ten miles. There are no cars."

Susan and I looked at each other in disbelief.

"Do they have airplane fuel?"

"This 1954 Piper Cub uses regular automobile gas. All they have at the airport is aviation fuel that my plane doesn't like. So, I fill up at the gas station."

I couldn't believe it. We were going to land a plane on the highway. On purpose. He's the Sheriff and will land anywhere he wants. Okay, this is going to be a good story. In the distance, I saw the gas station. Frank took the plane down on a long slow descent, not worrying about the length of the runway. I didn't even feel the wheels touch down. We slowed down and idled a few hundred yards to the Phillips 66 station. While Frank filled the plane with gasoline from a five gallon can, Susan and I took once in a lifetime photos of an airplane at a gas station, on purpose, with no damage. Then we climbed into the plane, saw no cars on the road, and took off down the highway. What an incredible ending to a fantastic week.

THE END

HOLE IN THE WALL

By Gordon England

"Kevin, the tuna are running hard. You need to come over to Nassau this weekend."

I faintly heard his reply through static on the phone connection from Nassau to Florida, "Count me in. I'll book a flight for Friday. Whose boat are we going on?"

I yelled back, "My friend, Doctor Neil from Jamaica, invited us to go on his twenty-six foot World Cat. You're gonna love it."

Kevin and I arrived at Dr. Greg Neil's house at sunrise, ready for a big day of deep water trolling. We were excited because Doc had heard of tuna caught only eight miles north of Nassau and I also had reports of fantastic catches of tuna at Hole in the Wall further north in the Abacos. I knew we were in for a great day fishing somewhere.

We pulled out of Nassau Harbor and met a ten knot southeast wind, meaning our original plan to run forty miles to the Exumas would be directly into strong wind and waves, so Doc chose Plan B and steered north on the leeward side of New Providence Island in calmer water. We trolled through dark blue Caribbean Sea until noon, with nary a strike. By then we were twelve miles offshore with winds building to fifteen knots.

Doc said, "Fish gone. Wanna make a move to Hole in the Wall?"

Kevin looked at me. "Why not? Let's go for it."

We pulled in our lines and began a thirty-eight-mile journey. Running with the wind, Doc pushed the throttles up to twenty knots with the catamaran's dual hulls slicing smoothly through moderate waves. An hour later we approached the thirty-mile wide Northeast Providence Channel between Eluthera and Abaco where the Atlantic makes a big swing westward, passing Grand Bahama, and on to the Gulf Stream toward Florida. The westerly current mixed with southeasterly winds created angry three to four foot chopped waves that only hardy sailors ventured through. Half way across the channel, the ragged, isolated Hole in the Wall cliffs at the southern tip of Abaco appeared above an angry sea. On top of the cliff, a lighthouse warned sailors of the abrupt change of deep water to hazardous rocks. Out of the corner of my eye I saw a big splash in the water at fifty yards.

I pointed. "Look over there." A huge fish jumped again completely out of the water, falling back with a splash.

Kevin said, "It must be a porpoise." The fish jumped repeatedly in a straight line, high into the air, hanging for a long second, and smoothly diving back with just a ripple.

"That's as big as a porpoise, but it's no porpoise," I exclaimed. "Its definitely a fish, but not a shark either."

Doc said, "That's a tuna." The fish jumped rapidly three more times moving away from us.

Kevin replied, "That's bigger than any yellowfin I ever saw. It's three or four hundred pounds."

In awe, I said, "Boys, that's a bluefin tuna. They used to be all over the islands, but now there's just a few left. Doc, do you wanna try to catch him?"

"No way. We don't have reels that big. He would just mash our gear. Let's keep going to Abaco."

A few miles later we came upon a massive, yellow weed line stretching one hundred feet wide as far as we could see. We trolled for dolphin along one side of the weeds with Islander skirted ballyhoo and in short order, Kevin brought in a fifteen-pound dolphin. After we dropped baits out again, an even larger dolphin hit and Doc took his turn at reeling. The dolphin, every bit of 30 pounds, tail-walked across the ocean in an attempt to escape.

I yelled, "Hang on Doc. Keep reeling. Don't let him get away."

Ten minutes into a hard fight on the bouncing boat, the fish was almost in range of the gaff. When it jumped high again, yellow and green flesh thrashing in anger, and splashed into the water, the hook broke loose and flew back into the boat, almost hitting Doc. We were crushed with disappointment that such a fine fish escaped.

While dolphin were fun to catch, our target for the day was tuna, so we pulled in our lines and continued in rough seas northward toward Hole in the Wall, one of the best spots in the

Bahamas for large tuna, dolphin, and marlin. A few hundred feet from the primordial cliffs, water depth dropped almost straight down 6,000 feet along an underwater wall. Two miles offshore an underwater ridge rose to six hundred feet below the surface, causing an upwelling where baitfish and predators congregated. That was where we hoped to strike paydirt.

When we trolled large ballyhoo across the ridge, one of the baits was slammed, bending the rod and causing the Penn International 50 reel to scream. I grabbed the rod while Doc put a fighting belt around my waist. The initial run took two hundred yards of line out in seconds.

Kevin exclaimed, "Its gotta be a wahoo!"

I held on until the fish slowed, then tightened the drag and started to fight. I slowly pumped and reeled a few inches of line at a time. When the rod tip jerked up and down, I recognized the pattern of a stubborn wahoo's headshake. Twenty minutes later I had the fish next to the boat where Kevin expertly gaffed a twenty-eight-pound wahoo and swung it into the fish box. We slammed the lid as the wildly thrashing fish pounded so violently that the fiberglass fish box tore loose from its floor mounts and fell down onto the gas tank. We put cushions between the box and gas tank and kept going.

After an hour with no more hits, I told Doc, "Its four o'clock and we have a fifty-one mile run against the wind. We better head back home. We'll come back next weekend for more."

Reluctantly, he turned south toward Nassau and told me, "You take the first shift. Kevin and I will take a break."

I took the wheel while they went below and attempted to sleep, but In rough seas, they bounced more than slept. Since we could only make seven or eight knots against the wind, I dropped a couple of marlin lures behind the boat. You never knew what lurked in these deep waters. If you didn't have a hook in the water you were guaranteed not to catch a fish. An hour and a half later, we were back on the original weed line halfway across the Channel. When our lures passed through the weeds, a rod bent and shook again.

I yelled, "Fish on!" waking the guys up.

Kevin scrambled back to the pitching stern, wrestled the rod out of the holder, and brought a twenty-five-pound barracuda to the boat.

Doc teased, "Kevin, why you catching de barry?"

They went back to sleep while I navigated southeast straight into wind-blown seas for two more hours until we left the Channel and found calmer water near Harbour Island on the north end of Eluthera. In the distance I saw a huge flock of brown noddy sea birds, locally called tuna birds, swirling in a frenzy, diving on small pieces of meat left by tuna tearing through baitfish.

I yelled, "Wake up guys. We got fish. There's also a frigate bird up high. Might be a marlin around here."

Kevin and Doc scrambled out of the cabin again and hurriedly changed baits to small, high-speed cedar plugs and plastic squid with eighty-pound fluorocarbon leaders. The fast moving tuna were hard to catch up with, so I sped up to fifteen knots, pounding through heavy waves. As we neared the birds, we saw hordes of tuna under them racing after baitfish. Inching in front of the school, I swung our lures in a large circle to intercept the fish, and then slowed down. Two rods went down simultaneously and line blistered off the reels. Doc and Kevin grabbed the rods, pumping and reeling while I steered to keep the fish behind the boat. In no time, we had two hard fighting, fifteen-pound yellowfin tuna in the boat.

After landing the tuna, we saw the birds again in the distance. Five more adrenaline filled minutes of pounding through crashing seas brought us to the birds again, where I pulled ahead of the school, and lines were dropped back. Wham, three rods bent angrily for a triple hook up. Chaos erupted on deck! Tuna crisscrossed each other in long powerful runs, entangling our lines and rods. We passed the rods around each other in a wild dance to keep lines untangled. I steered the boat and adjusted the throttle with one hand, holding my rod with the other hand. When I let go of the wheel to wind the reel, a wave caught us sideways and threw us around the boat like drunks as we laughed and cursed. When Doc brought his fish near the boat, I put my rod in a holder and picked up the gaff. Bending down to gaff the tuna, I saw a seven-foot long shadow pass beneath us.

I yelled, "Look at that marlin!"

I quickly brought Doc's skipjack tuna aboard and picked up my rod again. My fish fought hard for another five minutes and when it was thirty feet from the boat, my rod slammed down, the lure pulled free, and the line went limp. The marlin had taken my fish!

Meanwhile, Kevin still fought his tuna. Suddenly his rod went down hard and line peeled out as the marlin took off with Kevin's fish. The billfish was neon blue and white when it sky rocketed out of the water and tail walked above waves, shaking its head furiously, then splashed down, snapping the short, light tuna leader. Intimidated by the big fish's power, we stared in silence and realized much heavier reels and lines were needed to catch a mighty marlin.

The sun hung low and we still had a long run ahead of us. Our GPS showed Spanish Wells ten miles to the east in Eluthera.

I told Doc, "Lets head over toward Spanish Wells until we get into cell phone range where we call the wives. They'll be getting worried."

The rough sea and fading sky kept our speed down as we passed the island. I was not looking forward to a night run because you never knew what logs, ropes, reefs, or other boats awaited in the dark.

I said to Doc, "We could get a hotel over there and drive back in the morning."

He replied, "Naw, let's push on tonight."

"Its your boat, you have to drive in the dark in these treacherous reefs. I am not going to get blamed for wrecking your boat."

We couldn't see underwater reefs in the dark, but florescent white breakers would warn us of shallow reefs. Kevin worried about reefs in the dark, so he retreated to the cabin for the remainder of our voyage, while Doc and I stayed at the helm. When we picked up cell phone coverage three miles from Spanish Wells, Doc called his wife to notify her where we were, that we would be very late, and to call my wife.

Rather than take a straight, southerly course back across the open sea and rough water, we took a seventy-one mile curved route hugging the reef line for wind protection and better speed. We ran blind for three tortuous hours through a moonless night, smashing through waves, and following a GPS track through mazes of reefs past Atoll Island, Rose Island, Paradise Island, and Nassau. I stayed wide-awake, straining to see through darkness ahead of us. By now I was exhausted, running on overdrive from the long day; but there was no way I could go below and sleep.

When we reached the south side of Nassau to approach a narrow, unmarked channel to Doc's house, the GPS lost our track. The tide was low and we were blind and tired. Doc very slowly approached the shallow channel. Crunch. The boat jolted to a stop. Rats. The bow was firmly aground on a hard reef. I looked at Doc. One of us had to go overboard. I didn't want to tear up his props on the rocks, so I put on water shoes and slipped over the side into black, knee-deep water. I tried not to think about sharks, barracuda, or razor sharp coral. Ten feet behind the boat, waves rippled marking an edge of the deeper channel. Doc raised the engines and reversed them when I pushed on the bow. No good. The boat was too heavy. I waited for a small wave to gently raise the boat a few inches and then gave a big heave. The boat ground six inches backward across coral. I went into a cycle. Wait for another wave. Lift again, gaining a few more inches backward. When I took my next step forward, my foot went into a hole of sharp coral, cutting my shin. Damn blood. Sharks hunt at night. I kept pushing. I gained a few more feet, finally breaking the boat loose into deeper water. That's when a gust of wind grabbed the stern and swung it around. Crunch again. This time the boat was crossways to the wind with the whole bottom grinding on coral with each passing wave.

Doc asked, "Hey buddy. You okay?"

"Yeah, gotta start over. I'm sure am glad it's not my boat." I slowly waded back to the stern, my mind in a fog, gingerly checking with each step to avoid more holes. With the next rising wave I walked the stern out to the edge of the channel.

"Doc, it is deeper back here. Drop the engines a little and see if you can pull us off this damn reef."

The propellers grabbed enough water to keep the wind from swinging the boat around again. Back to the bow I walked. Tired. Back hurts. Start the cycle again. Push, step. Push, step. Inch by inch we worked the boat back to the channel, finally pulling free. I grabbed the rail when Doc gunned the engine, struggling to pull myself up into the boat. I fell onto the deck in exhaustion.

At long last, we pulled into Doc's dock at eleven thirty, relieved to be back on solid land. After two more hours of cleaning the boat and fish, Kevin and I made the thirty-minute ride home, completely zoned out. I was glad there was no traffic on the read. By the time we refrigerated the fish and cleaned up, it was three o'clock. Kevin and I called it a day and hit the sack exhausted, dreaming of the marlin that got away in the wild Sea of Abaco.

THE END

THE OTHER SIDE

By Gordon England

Gordon said to Annie, "Guess where we're going Saturday."

"Tell me."

"Fishing on Ron Sparks' new thirty-six foot Delta, the Perseverance. We're going to the other-side."

"The other side of what?"

"The other side of the Gulf Stream. Yellowfin, bonita, and skipjack tuna stay sixty to a hundred miles offshore. Only the big boats go after them because you gotta have lots of gas and be able to handle big seas on this trip."

"Who's going with us?"

"Lou Ziazas and his son, Troy. Lou's been fishing for years on his own boat. He's gonna train us rookies."

"Wow, this will be a big adventure. I'll start planning the food. I can make lots of sandwiches," Annie said with a big smile.

When Annie and Gordon showed up at Harbor Town Marina in Port Canaveral at three o'clock Saturday morning, Ron already had the engines warmed up.

Gordon shouted, "Ahoy!" Ron climbed out of the engine compartment.

"Come aboard and look at these new twin Caterpillar 3208's."

Gordon looked under the hatch and exclaimed, "They're gorgeous. The whole engine room is spotless. I'd expected nothing less from an engineer like you."

"Lou, show them where to stow their gear."

Annie said, "I brought plenty of food."

Lou replied, "I'm glad you came along. There's a refrigerator down in the cabin."

"I'll go down below and organize the galley."

A long distance run to the other-side required more gear and supplies than a normal fishing trip. Gordon helped stow ten bags of ice, six twelve-packs of frozen ballyhoo, four rods with gold Penn International 50 reels, and a bucket full of trolling lures.

At three-thirty Ron ordered, "Cast the lines. We got an appointment with tuna at daybreak. Can't be late."

When Lou pushed Perseverance away from the dock, we were the only boat moving in the darkness. Ron idled smooth as a ghost through still waters of the port. Our wavelets rippled quietly into boats and seawalls. Familiar smells of salt, shrimp boats, and diesel wafted across the water, triggering deep memories from Gordon's past fishing journeys. He wondered what today would hold.

Once past the port's entrance, Ron turned eastward and pushed the boat up to cruising speed of twenty-one knots. The deep bow cut through the glassy ocean like butter. Gordon and Annie climbed the ladder from the deck up to the dark flybridge where Ron sat at the wheel. His console had a few lit gauges and an early model Loran with a numeric screen. Gordon noted there were no directional electronics or lit compass on the dash.

He asked, "How do you know where you're going?"

"We just head east until we find fish. To come back we head west, can't miss Florida. I didn't have time to activate the light on the compass, but don't worry, once the sun comes up we can see it." Gordon glanced sideways at Annie with raised eyebrows.

He asked, "How do you know where we are?"

"From the latitude and longitude on the loran I can find where we are on the chart. I know the coordinates for the port, so I can steer my way back, no problem."

"You're kidding. You calculate the course by watching the lat longs change?"

"Long numbers are east-west and latitude numbers are north-south. I've been doing that for years. We're in the shipping lanes, so help me watch for other boats. They're supposed to have their lights on, but you never know."

Gordon turned to Annie, "At this speed we couldn't see a dark boat until we hit it. This night running is spooky business. Oh the heck with it. We're having fun now."

He asked, "How long does it take to get to the other- side?"

"We'll have a three hour run. Why don't you go help Lou rig lures? Annie, stay up here and help me watch for boats. Be sure to give me plenty of warning if you see anything."

Gordon laughed. "Yeah Annie, give Ron plenty of warning." He climbed down the ladder to join the rest of the crew.

An hour later a color change of the water and two-foot ripples indicated they had entered the Gulf Stream. Two-foot waves were no match for the superbly designed hull of Perseverance. Ron continued eastward another two hours while the crew rigged baits, lines, rods, and saved energy for big action. Since Gordon and Troy were too excited to sleep, Lou primed them about fast tuna action.

"We'll be running and gunning at high speed all day. Tuna chase schools of pilchards, so we watch for swarms of birds scavenging pieces of bait left by tuna. We'll drag ballyhoo with skirts. When we see birds, we speed up ahead of the school and then slow down to let them intercept our lures. Bonita run five to ten pounds, but yellowfins get up to one hundred pounds or more. They're the hardest fighting fish in the sea. Are you ready?"

Gordon replied, "I was born ready. You just find the fish."

Annie went below and soon emerged with coffee and doughnuts as the faint light of sunrise peeked through black night ahead of us.

She announced, "You better eat now, we'll be fishing soon."

Gordon looked at Lou. "Annie's gonna keep us well fed today."

The sun broke the edge of the sea in a thin, gold sliver, revealing the sea flattened out smooth as glass.

Ron yelled to the crew, "Okay guys. We just left the Gulf Stream. Lou, you got everything ready?"

"Aye-aye Captain. Rods are rigged and bait is ready. Troy, go up in the tuna tower and look for birds."

Ron zigzagged eastward at sixteen knots to maximize coverage of the ocean.

An hour later we heard Troy yell, "Birds at ten o'clock." Ron turned the boat toward a flock of birds a half-mile away and the fire drill started. A melee of fifty plus white terns swirled and dove on baitfish that jumped out of the water to escape murderous tuna attacking from below. Yellowfins jumped completely out of the water to catch fleeing pilchards in midair. The awesome frenzy of fish, birds, and pilchards moved at fifteen knots.

Ron sped up to twenty knots on a parallel course. When he pulled ahead of the school, baits were dropped in front of a riot of fish and birds. He backed off the throttle, allowing the fish to catch up to the lures. The crew braced for battle. Thrashing fish approached the lures, sensed the boat, and turned left, ignoring the baits. Ron sped ahead of the school again, swerved left, and slowed down. The tuna spooked again and disappeared into deep blue water.

Ron circled for fifteen minutes, then spotted the birds a mile to the northeast. He raced in, but the fish sounded before baits were even put in the water.

This set the pattern for the remainder of the day. Run at high-speed north and east until birds were sighted, race after them, make one or two passes through the fish with the lures, no bites, and then the fish would sound without touching the baits. By three o'clock the crew was tired of chasing fish with lockjaw.

Lou asked Ron, "How far out are we?"

"Just a minute, let me calculate. Hmmm. About eighty miles."

"And how far north?"

"Hmmm. We're off New Smyrna Beach."

Lou replied, "We gotta long run back home. I've had all the fun I can stand. What do you say we head back guys? I see clouds building in the west." Ron agreed and turned southwest.

Five minutes later Gordon shouted, "Birds at two o'clock."

Ron steered toward the swarm of birds while the crew grabbed rods and dropped baits one more time. When the lures passed through the school of fish, the shotgun line received a powerful hit that bent the heavy rod almost double. Gordon reached to the overhead rocket launcher and struggled to remove the bucking rod. He jammed the rod butt into his stomach and watched line screamed off the reel. This was Gordon's first large fish and he didn't know how much abuse his reel could take before it melted.

Lou yelled, "That's a big fish. He hasn't slowed down yet. Troy, get a fighting belt for Gordon. Ron, chase that fish before he spools the reel." The rest of the crew quickly reeled in the other lines while Gordon waited for the run to stop before he tightened the drag and cranked on the reel. Ron turned the boat and slowly gained on the tuna while Gordon struggled to reel line.

Lou commanded, "Don't pump with your arms, use your legs and back. Tighten up the drag a bit."

"I can't stop him, he's huge." Gordon sat on the ice chest and braced his feet against the rail while the tuna dove deep, taking out more line.

He complained, "Ron, you need a fighting chair in this boat. God this is a big fish."

"Keep reeling, unless you want Troy to take the rod."

"No way. That's my fish."

Gordon pumped and reeled, pumped and reeled, gaining line back inches at a time. Every time the tuna changed direction the ice chest slid across the deck and slammed Gordon into the opposite rail. After thirty minutes, his arms and back were wracked with cramps and his hands were locked into claws. He reeled by moving his arms up and down. He was more exhausted than he had ever been, but was not about to give up. Annie poured cold water on his face and offered words of encouragement.

Lou yelled, "Don't stop reeling," every time Gordon slowed to rest. To keep the tuna from circling the boat, Ron motored forward at three knots, adding more pull to the line.

Lou exclaimed, "I see color. He's coming up. Stand over here to the port side where I can gaff in front of you. Troy, open the fish box."

Gordon grunted, rose off the ice chest, and staggered to the rail. At last he saw the fish causing him so much pain. The amazing beast was five feet long, over one hundred pounds. Yellow pectoral fins extended twelve inches on each side. A powerful tail pulsated from side to side.

Troy said, "Pull him in closer."

"I'm trying, but my arms are killing me,"

"Keep reeling, he's almost here. Ron, a little more to the left."

Gordon struggled to bring the fish into range of the gaff. The fish rolled onto its side, looking up defiantly with a large black eye. Lou slammed the six-foot metal gaff into the tuna and attempted to lift it into the boat. That's when he realized he had underestimated the size and strength of the fish. The tuna exploded in fury, shaking its head back and forth in a frenzy that pulled Lou downward. Lou grunted and tried to lift again, but the fish was too heavy. The gaff shook violently and broke free from Lou's hands. The end of the gaff now whipped back and forth, severely pounding Lou's arms. He howled and jumped back. The tuna dove under the boat. Gordon was jerked down, his rod near the water. When the gaff disappeared into the frothing sea, the line broke free, causing Gordon to tumble backwards.

Whack whack whack. A loud noise came from the bottom of the boat.

Lou screamed, "Stop."

Ron killed the engines to stop the dreadful noise. Blood boiled up from the stern. The crew stared at each other in disbelief. Lou was really pissed and hurt.

He moaned, "I couldn't hold on. The gaff beat me up."

Ron asked, "Are your arms broken?"

"No. But they hurt like hell."

Annie anxiously asked, "What was all that noise?"

Ron replied, "I don't know, but it wasn't good."

"What are we going to do?"

"Troy, go into the locker in the galley. See if you can find a mask and snorkel. Lets clear the deck so I can go overboard to see what the problem is."

The crew stared at each other in disbelief. The adrenaline of the long fight still prevented clear thought. Broken down at eighty miles out. This was no longer fun.

Troy climbed out of the cabin and reported, "I found two masks and a snorkel." He looked over the stern, "Do you have a dive ladder?"

Ron replied, "No, but there's a dive platform."

"Oh."

Ron put on a mask and snorkel and stepped over the transom onto the dive platform.

"I'll go underneath and check the prop."

The slick ocean of the morning had changed to three feet seas with the advancing clouds. The stilled boat swung crossways to the waves, rocking back and forth. Ron dove under the boat while Gordon sat down in exhaustion and stared at Annie.

She nervously said, "I can't believe he dove into all that blood. There's gonna be sharks." Jaws had given her a deep terror of sharks.

Gordon said, "Your job is to watch for sharks while we fix the boat."

Annie's took her post at the stern. With wide eyes she stared into the bottomless blue water for approaching fins. Ron popped out of the water and crawled up onto the dive platform.

Troy asked, "What did you see?"

"We have a problem. The gaff is wrapped around the port drive shaft and the line and wire leader is wrapped all around the propeller. Of course, the fish is gone."

The crew was stunned. Not only had they lost the fish, the fish had crippled the boat.

"We gotta clear this mess or limp home on one motor at slow speed. Troy, go down below and find my toolbox. I need the wire cutters so I can get the wire off the prop. Lou, come help me under the boat."

When Troy brought the wire cutters, Lou put on a mask and joined Ron in the water to dive under the bobbing boat.

Thirty-seconds later they surfaced and placed a handful of line on the platform. Down they went again. And again. Each time removing more wire and line from the prop. Each dive under the boat was shorter as they quickly tired out. After ten minutes, they climbed back on the platform and into the boat. They sat for a minute to regain their strength.

Gordon asked, "How's it look?"

Ron replied, "We got all the line and wire off. Now we gotta get the gaff off the drive shaft. Hand me the big pliers. I don't want this damn snorkel. I can't breath when the waves break over it."

They climbed back overboard and dove under the boat. After a minute, they surfaced, grabbed the rocking platform, caught their breath, and went back down again while Annie continued her vigil for sharks. Several dives later they came back up and struggled onto the platform. Bleak looks on their faces foretold more problems.

Ron caught his breath and said, "When I grab the gaff with the pliers, it just spins. Gordon, give us the pipe wrench. Troy, you hold the gaff with the pipe wrench and I'll try to break it off with the pliers." Gordon handed the five-pound wrench to Troy. Back down under the boat went Ron and Troy.

Gordon told Annie, "That's gotta be tough. When I scuba dive with five pounds of weights I sink to the bottom."

She grimly shook her head as she watched for sharks.

They surfaced twenty seconds later, gasped for air, then went back down again. When they came back up the next time they threw the pliers, pipe wrench, and a two foot piece of the crooked, one-inch diameter gaff onto the platform. They struggled back on board exhausted.

After a few minutes of hard breathing, Ron said, "Even with both tools, the gaff spins. I can't do this any more. Is there a hacksaw in the tool box?"

Gordon looked in the box and replied, "No."

"Go down in the engine compartment and see if you can find a hack saw." Gordon searched the engine room and the cabin. No hack saw.

Ron dejectedly said, "Okay Lou, see what you can do."

Lou dove into the water and spent the next ten minutes going under for thirty seconds, coming back up for air, then disappearing under the boat again. He finally dragged himself onto the platform, laboring for breath.

He shook his head and gasped, "I loosened it up some, but I can't break it off."

Ron looked at Gordon. "Your turn."

Annie gave Gordon a pained look when he put on the mask and jumped overboard. He looked down into an endless, deep blue abyss streaked with silver rays of sunlight. He saw at least one hundred feet down into nothing. Visions of sharks or some unimaginable creature rising from the depths struck a primordial fear in his mind. He raised his head above the surface and grabbed a breath, deciding not to look down again.

Gordon dove under the boat, grabbed the propeller, and pulled himself toward the inboard drive shaft. The bottom of the boat moved up and down three feet every few seconds. He saw the gold gaff spiraled around the shaft like spaghetti. When he grabbed it and pulled, it just spun in a circle. He pulled again. Nothing.

Gordon kicked back to the surface, took a couple of breaths of air, and dove back under the boat. He turned upside down, placed his feet against the bottom of the bucking boat, and pulled down on the end of the gaff. The shaft had a weak spot where it creased twelve inches from the end. The end of the gaff moved out an inch, straightening at the crease. The boat rose and slammed back down, causing Gordon's feet to slip. The boat banged his hip. When he yelled in pain, his air bubbled out. He pushed away, rose to the surface, and swam to the dive platform. He held on for a minute to catch his breath and then repeated the drill. He braced his feet on the bottom of the boat again and gave a big pull, breaking off the end of the gaff at the crease. He swam back to the surface and handed the foot long piece of gaff to Annie. Gordon was really exhausted. He held onto the bouncing platform, struggling for breath. After two more dives under the boat, he could dive no more. He crawled onto the platform and lay there for a minute to rest. Lou gave him a hand and pulled him back into the boat.

Ron asked, "What does it look like?"

Gordon replied haltingly, "I loosened it a bit more, but there's still three-feet of gaff wound loosely around the shaft. That's all I can do."

The exhausted crew pondered the situation grimly. They had struggled with the gaff for an hour. No one had the energy to dive under the boat again. It was now six o'clock. Dark clouds were building in the west.

Lou asked Ron, "Can you reach anyone on the radio?"

"No, we're too far out."

"Why don't you start the engines and see what happens."

"Good idea."

Ron turned on the motors and gently placed both engines into gear. Everyone held their breath. No knocking. He increased the rpms. Nothing. He increased speed to ten knots. Nothing. At fifteen knots and they heard a light tap of the gaff hitting the bottom of the boat. He backed off the throttle slightly until the tapping stopped.

With a grin Ron said, "I think we're going to be okay."

The crew breathed a big sigh of relief; glad they were not going to spend the night on the boat waiting to be rescued. Ron turned southwest toward the port. Annie went to the cabin and emerged shortly with sandwiches for the worn out crew.

It was seven o'clock when they approached a wall of black clouds stretching far to the south. The seas had built to five feet, limiting speed to ten knots into the waves. Ron had no choice but to push through the storm toward home. Rough waves made it impossible to stay in the cabin, so Annie and Gordon sat on two seats on the flybridge next to the captain's chair. Lou and Troy stood on the deck and held onto rails, struggling for balance with each rolling wave. Dark clouds brought an early sunset. A while later, Ron turned the boat and drove slowly downwind for a brief smooth ride.

He told Lou, "Secure the cabin, it's going to be a long night. Bring out the life jackets and spread them on the deck to make a bed to lie on. Troy, look in the drawer under the bunk and find a flashlight. We'll need that for navigating. Anybody needs a pit stop, now is the time. Annie, if you got any coffee left? I sure could use some."

Annie brought him coffee and asked, "How far out are we?"

Ron paused, looked at the loran, and made a mental calculation. "About forty miles."

The crew looked at each other and grimaced. They cleared the deck of rods, rigs, and loose gear, securing the boat for rough riding. Lou, Troy, and Annie lay down on the life jackets.

Gordon climbed up to the flybridge with Ron and reported, "We're ready to go Captain."

Ron replied, "I can navigate roughly with the loran numbers, but the compass is better. You'll have to shine the flashlight on the compass to help me steer the course. The batteries won't last all night, so just turn the flashlight on every few minutes to take a reading."

"Aye aye, captain."

He turned Perseverance around and quartered on a southwest course against the westerly waves. Five-foot waves at four-second intervals took control of the boat, demanding full concentration from Gordon and Ron. Ron worked the dual throttles continuously with his right hand. He accelerated up the face of each wave, then slowed down at the top to avoid racing down the backside and pitchpoling at the bottom. His left hand on the wheel jerked back and forth on the wheel to ensure the boat reached the top of the waves at ninety degrees to avoid being broadsided. Then he steered slightly to the left on the backside of the waves to maintain an average southwesterly heading. At the same time, he watched the loran numbers change and calculated the course heading. The boat bucked violently, preventing Gordon and Ron from sitting in the chairs to operate the controls, so they stood and bent their legs constantly to adjust to the pitching floor. Gordon turned on the flashlight every few minutes to get a compass heading in case Ron's math slipped.

Downstairs, the crew found the only way to lie on the deck was with their feet facing the stern. The life jackets slid toward the back of the boat every time they went up the face of a wave. The crew used their feet to push themselves off the transom. There was also an easterly tailwind that blew noxious diesel fumes back onto deck, causing Annie to feel sick. She periodically staggered up the stairs to get fresh air and calm her stomach.

Nobody slept during this voyage, they just endured. The only saving grace was that no rain fell that night, although the crew was still soaked from waves breaking over the gunnels.

After thirty minutes at the wheel, Ron yelled to Gordon over the noise of the wind and diesels, "Let's switch."

"I don't know how to do this."

"I need a break. I'll show you how."

They waited until they were at the bottom of a wave, then quickly traded places. Gordon grabbed the wheel and adjusted the throttles just as a wave passed under them.

"Whoa. This isn't like driving my little eighteen-footer."

"Watch the tachometers and keep both engines at the same rpm. I'll watch the loran and tell you which direction to steer. Head directly into the waves when they break or we might get rolled."

Gordon grimly settled into a zone, completely concentrating on navigating the boat. Every time Ron turned on the flashlight to check the compass, Gordon's night vision was ruined. Thirty minutes later he was exhausted for the third time that day.

He told Ron, "I gotta quit."

"Okay, give me the wheel and go tell Lou to come up for a while." Gordon climbed down the bouncing stairs and collapsed on the deck.

"Lou, it's your turn. I hope you can read loran numbers."

For the next three and a half hours the crew rotated between driving the boat and lying on the deck sucking noxious diesel fumes. Progress was slow against the Gulf Stream and rough waves. Fatigue set in. The shifts grew shorter. At twenty miles from Port Canaveral, the crew was relieved to see the beam from the Cape Canaveral lighthouse four miles north of the Port. They no longer had to struggle to watch the loran numbers change and hold a course based on the compass.

An hour later Gordon was at the wheel with Lou at his side. Once he passed the lighthouse he planned to make a westerly turn into port, but it seemed the lighthouse was an elusive ghost that stayed in front of them no matter how long they rode.

They rose to the top of a wave and Lou yelled, "Breakers at two o'clock! Turn left!"

They were approaching the Cape Canaveral Shoals at the False Cape, a one to two fathom deep ridge that extended four miles northeast of the tip of the Cape. These shoals were legendary among sailors for sinking ships with massive waves.

Gordon swung the wheel just as a monster wave caught them broadside, throwing the crew across the boat. Perseverance rolled forty-five degrees, then righted herself like a cork.

Ron staggered up the stairs, "What the hell happened?"

Lou pointed, "The shoals!"

Gordon asked Ron, "Can you tell how far offshore we are?"

"No."

"Do you know how far the shoals come out?

"No."

"You take the wheel. I don't want to wreck your boat."

He passed the wheel to Ron as another wave broke over the boat and drenched the crew. They yelled and scrambled to their feet, a surge of adrenaline bringing them out of their stupor. They watched the thunderous, white breakers in the dark, fifty yards to starboard. Shallow water caused the ocean's swells to rise up and become very sloppy, tossing the boat like flotsam.

Ron took the wheel and turned the boat southeast, parallel to the breakers. Time after time waves broke over the side of the boat. The crew struggled not to be washed overboard. Gradually Ron pulled away from the shoals.

Gordon yelled, "How do we get back?"

"We go due south until the lighthouse is behind us, then we turn west and follow the buoy line into the port."

"I've been watching that damn lighthouse for hours. I don't think this day will ever end."

"Watch out for more breakers."

"I'm toasted, I'm going to the deck to rest again."

An hour later they finally passed the lighthouse. Ron turned westward at a flashing channel buoy, lining up for the final three miles into rough wind. The waves were no longer five footers. Instead, shallow water caused three-foot chop in all directions. At long last, Perseverance entered calmer waters of the port. However, Ron faced one last challenge of getting the boat into its slip.

Ron ordered, "Lou and Troy, bring out the lines, fenders, and boathooks. I have to turn the boat broadside to the wind and back into the slip. I have only done this in daylight, not in the dark."

Lou asked Ron, "How do I turn on the spreader lights?"

"I don't have them hooked up yet. Gordon and Annie, use the flashlights to guide us in."

Annie looked at Gordon and moaned, "Is this day ever going to end?"

Ron swung the boat around and attempted to back into the slip. A dual engine boat is steered backwards by using the throttles independently, unlike moving forward and steering with the rudder. Increasing the speed of one motor in reverse turns the boat in the opposite direction. The motors pull a boat backwards, causing the front of the boat to swing around like a car having the steering wheel move the rear wheels instead of the front. When Ron pointed the stern at the mouth of the slip and throttled backwards, strong wind pushed the boat sideways past the slip's piling. Gordon's flashlight showed the boat heading right at the piling.

"Stop! Go forward!" Ron shifted the motors into forward and goosed the throttles, jerking the crew across the deck. The boat surged ahead just before hitting the piling. He swung the boat around and tried again. Once again the crosswind pushed the boat out of position. After the long ride, Ron's foggy brain was not working well.

For twenty minutes he repeatedly attempted to bring his boat the last few feet home. Twice he had the boat half way in, only to have the wind twist the boat against the pilings and scrape the sides. The crew was too exhausted to push the boat away from the pilings. Ron pulled back and tried again. After coming so far and so long, the crew watched helplessly, hoping Ron could maneuver Perseverance into the slip and end the trip.

Finally a mate from another boat walked out onto the pier and asked, "You boys need some help?"

"Sure do," replied Lou. "This crosswind's a bitch."

"Throw me a line and I'll guide you in."

With the mate's help they finally brought the boat into the slip and tied it down. The crew stumbled onto the dock in a daze, not believing they were on solid ground. Their twenty-hour ordeal was finally over.

THE END

FATHER'S EYES

By Sudeshna Majumdar

This story is about a skinny young boy who loved football with all his heart. Practice after practice, he eagerly gave everything he had. But being half the size of the other boys, he got absolutely nowhere. At all the games, this hopeful athlete sat on the bench and hardly ever played. This teenager lived alone with his father, and the two of them had a very special relationship. Even though the son was always on the bench, his father was always in the stands cheering. He never missed a game. This young man was still the smallest of the class when he entered high school. But his father continued to encourage him but also made it very clear that he did not have to play football if he didn't want to. But the young man loved football and decided to hang in there. He was determined to try his best at every practice, and perhaps he'd get to play when he became a senior.

All through high school he never missed a practice or a game but remained a bench-warmer all four years. His faithful father was always in the stands, always with words of encouragement for him. When the young man went to college, he decided to try out for the football team as a walk-on. Everyone was sure he could never make the cut, but he did. The coach admitted that he kept him on the roster because he always puts his heart and soul to every practice, and at the same time, provided the other members with the spirit and hustle they badly needed. The news that he had survived the cut thrilled him so much that he rushed to the nearest phone and called his father. His father shared the son's excitement and received season tickets for all the college games.

This persistent young athlete never missed practice during his four years at college, but he never got to play in a game. It was the end of his senior football season, and as he trotted onto the practice field shortly before the big playoff game, the coach met him with a telegram. The young man read the telegram and he became deathly silent. Swallowing hard, he mumbled to the coach, "My father died this morning. Is it all right if I miss practice today"? The coach put his arm gently around his shoulder and said, "Take the rest of the week off, son. And don't even plan to come back to the game on Saturday."

Saturday arrived, and the game was not going well. In the third quarter, when the team was ten points behind, a silent young man quietly slipped into the empty locker room and put on his football gear.

As he ran onto the sidelines, the coach and his players were astounded to see their faithful team-mate back so soon. "Coach, please let me play. I've just got to play today," said the young man. The coach pretended not to hear him. There was no way he wanted his worst player in this close playoff game. But the young man persisted, and finally, feeling sorry for the kid, the coach gave in. "All right," he said. "22 You can go in." Before long, the coach, the players, and everyone in the stands could not believe their eyes. This little unknown, who had never played before, was doing everything right. The opposing team could not stop him.

He ran, he passed, blocked, and tackled like a star. His team began to triumph. The score was soon tied.

In the closing seconds of the game, this kid intercepted a pass and ran all the way for the winning touchdown. The fans broke loose. His team-mates hoisted him onto their shoulders. Such cheering you never heard.

Finally, after the stands had emptied and the team had showered and left the locker room, the coach noticed that this young man was sitting quietly in the corner all alone. The coach came to him and said, "Kid, I can't believe it. You were fantastic! Tell me, what got into you? How did you do it?" The young man looked at the coach with tears in his eyes and said, "Well, you knew my dad died, but did you know that my dad was blind?" The young man swallowed hard and forced a smile, "Dad came to all my games, but today was the first time he could see me play and I wanted to show him I could do it."

THE END

Made in United States
North Haven, CT
11 November 2021